WAGONS
WEST TO
MONTANA

Emma Jo Olson Heimark Renner

Order this book online at www.trafford.com
or email orders@trafford.com

Most Trafford titles are also available at major online book retailers.

Printed in the United States of America.

ISBN: 978-1-4907-0924-6 (sc)
ISBN: 978-1-4907-0923-9 (e)

Trafford rev. 07/29/2013

 www.trafford.com

North America & international
toll-free: 1 888 232 4444 (USA & Canada)
fax: 812 355 4082

This novel is dedicated to my sis and my children and grand children and great grand children, my dear family who make me proud and give me great joy.

List of Characters

James Larson	
Tom Larson	
Wife	Rosalea
Parents	John and Mary Boreson
Daughter	Dawn
John Obey	
Wife	Lilly
Sons	Josh and Jereme
Jess Logan	wagon master
The Dabbs	with the wagon train
Will Culbert	Culbert's Corner store owner
Dan Culbert	Culbert's Corner
Molly Craft	Boarding house, diner at Culbert's Corner
Jonathan Brooks	Minister at Culbert's Corner
Wife	Saraha Teacher
Joe Ames	Rancher
Tony Ogerly	Rancher
Son	Pete
Son	Paul
Rock, just Rock	Ranch hand
Danny	Orphan

CHAPTER 1

"West we will go, by wagons west to Montana territory. A week from today we will start on our way! The train will pick up the cars carrying our wagons, horses, and all the rest of our things, and take us to the end of the track. There, we will become a part of the next wagon train that forms up and we will head west."

The speaker was James Larson. There was excitement in his voice reflecting the earnestness of the anticipation of the coming trip to a ranch out west. It was the ranch that he had founded and worked to make productive. In time it would be a big ranch where they could have many cattle and horses. The ranch was on a great open area of thousands of acres of grassland waiting for ranchers to make their homes.

His brother Tom's family, his wife Rosalea and daughter Dawn, were going with him, west to Montana. They would be joining him to make their home on the ranch in the far west.

The tall blond man, with his hand touching the side of the window, stood looking out to the western sky. Thinking of the ranch far away, on the rolling grassland. The view from the ranch had high mountains that stood tall off to the west. The view to the north, east and even southward, it was a vast rolling grass covered prairie. A river and streams crossed the ranch and wandering on out of sight to the east.

He had told them of that land and the mountains, describing eagerly it all from the best of his remembrance. His enthusiasm had colored the descriptions, trying to make them seem real. It was wild open prairie with range after range of tall grass, grass in abundance everywhere. There were places where there were streams and rivers with their breaks and canyons. The canyons were filled with trees and bushes. Wild life was living everywhere they pleased. There were many kinds of birds as well as elk, deer, antelope and even buffalo. All this he had told them.

In his search in of the vast area, he had found a ranch, populated with the one family with the father and mother of two girls and 4 sons, all young, but nearly adults. They had spent three years working on that ranch and liked and admired the family. Although it was hard work at times, he enjoyed the life. He was glad for the time of learning with the friendship, advice, and support of the Rancher.

Had a tall black haired girl begun to come to his mind more and more often, he wondered. Her black hair shining in the sun. Eyes the deepest blue that he had ever seen. A deep blue of almost purple. She was slender and sat in the saddle like she had been born there. Her laugh was like the music of the stream running over the rocks. A happy sound.

He checked his thoughts. He groaned inwardly and mentally shook his head. These kind of thoughts will have to wait for another day.

Back to the discussion. Turning around he smiled as he continued.

"Here, in the east, we can own 10 acres, some places, maybe 100. Out there we can have 1,000-10,000, 20,000 or more acres. It is all open range, no one living for many miles in any direction.

There is another ranch about 10 miles away," he told them. "And another farther away, probably 50 miles. We will be in a partnership with John Obey. Even with the two lads and Rock, our cook, there is only 6 of us men. We could have it tough. Because of the work and us not having a crew of riders, the winters especially, could be bad until we can find some riders to work for us." He stopped and took a sip of his coffee.

Then continued; "We can have cattle, and horses, raise grain and corn. We can have a big garden. Raise almost everything that we need. We can be pretty much independent, not depending on anyone for much of anything, with but a few exceptions. One of the best things, spring usually comes early and summer lingers well into fall, good for gardens and grains."

He had described not only the beauty of the area, but the many advantages available, thus he had tried to convince them. It really hadn't been hard to convince them, the descriptions and possibilities had intrigued them. A new way of life had called to them. They had responded and were anxious and nearly ready to go. The last purchases soon to be completed. Then the final packing and all would be loaded into the train cars that already awaited them.

"We will soon be heading out, on our way to that new home. It is a long way, a long trip, and will take about 4 months if all goes well. Maybe 5 months if there are storms and rains soaking up the ground into mud. If we can start with the wagon train by the first of May, we should get to the ranch by the end of August," he said as he sat down.

They were sitting around the table, coffee cups before them, finalizing the plans for the long trip west. This would be the last time to discus the trip in depth, so that they all would know what to expect and what to do in the final preparations before they left. James Larson, like his brother Tom, more than 6 ft tall, broad shouldered, dark blond hair with blue/grey eyes. Both were ruggedly good looking, strong men. Lips that could smile, and laugh with voices mildly soft except when needed to be strong, then their voices carried, penetrating with convincing authority. Both men were known and admired as friends by all who knew them. They would be missed in the community.

James continued; "This will be my third trip west. I know that we have talked about this before, but I want to be sure that we all know what to expect and be prepared for the trip.

"We take the train to Independence Missouri. There we will join a wagon train and travel west, the same trail that I have traveled before. I know the way, but even so, there may different things happening. There is much work to be done every day on the trip. Animals to be taken care of, wagon wheels need greasing often. Harness checked for repairs. A wagon may break down and we have to take time to fix it. We can't leave someone stranded on the prairie. Rarely, but sometimes an animal gets sick or hurt, maybe dies. People get hurt or sick. Even a baby may be born on the way. Oh, wagon wheels come off, or break. It has happened, and maybe will again.

"We seldom see Indians; mostly mid/west with the Lakota, Sioux. And farther west, in the Montana territory, there are Black Foot and Flathead. We have found them friendly when we do see them. Or they appear to ignore us. That doesn't mean that trouble won't break out again. Hopefully it won't. The days of the trouble with the Indians is over we believe, and hope. They are mostly good people.

"Sometimes there is a disturbance between people on the wagon train, but not often. Mostly we help each other and we have good times and things should go well. Don't be mistaken; it will be a long, hard, trying trip. We will get tired, Very tired before we toughen up or get there. Some may get discouraged at the length of time the trip takes. Some may even turn back.

"There is much beauty in many places along the way. The prairie has a beauty all it's own. There are places where the prairie seems endless, almost level, rolling on and on. There is no wood for miles and buffalo chips will have to be used for cooking fires. There are streams and rivers we have to cross, where trees and bushes grow. Then it may be days before we see a tree or even brush until we get to the sagebrush country and sage takes over the land for miles. The sage and prairie grass has a beauty all it's own and wild flowers may be found almost everywhere this time of the year and all summer with many fall flowers. We may have rain, maybe several times. There can be storms with hard rain. Yes, we may even have a snow storm, but not so likely by the time we go. And hopefully we will be home in Montana before winter storms start."

"There are many wild animals. We should see many antelope and deer and there may be some buffalo, but not so many any more. Back on our ranch we may see deer and elk. Elk are like deer only bigger. There are smaller animals too. Prairie dogs, Badgers sometimes. There may be beaver dams on rivers or even small streams. Coyotes and rarely a wolf, but seldom seen in the day time. We may hear them during the night. There are fish in many of the streams and rivers, some of us can take time in the evenings to catch a few. And the fish will be a welcome change."

"There is an exodus, a migration of people from the east, going west. Every year more people are moving out into the new country, where it is open and they can own more land. There is place and room where they can be independent to make homes and have families.

"All along the way, there is a lot of open land with no one living for many miles. Some places, some will find a place that they like and stop there to make their home, to farm, to raise grains and gardens. Most will have horses, and of course, milk cows, chickens, maybe hogs and sheep. People will move out to the west and find a place to live and make new homes. We are going to be some of the first to settle far to the west on the high range, cattle country. Farther on to the west is the Oregon Territory along a great river, and in California with the gold mines, and far, the Pacific Ocean.

"We hope that we may be early enough to get to the end of the track before many others of the travelers get there this spring. Maybe we will be part of a smaller group joining the first wagon train to go west this season. That is what I hope. Later in the season the wagon trains will be larger as more people are moving west. Even a small group, like we may be in, should go through well. Our wagons and equipment are new and our horses are young and strong, some of the best. Hopefully the others in the group of the wagon train will be too. We are all young and healthy and should stay healthy. Oh there maybe older people in our group too, but if they are going west, they will know what to expect. Every thing should go well and we should have a good trip."

James grinned, "The problem that we may have is that there are few girls and women in the west and there will be cowboys and ranchers who will want to marry our girl, Dawn. We will have to watch that there is no one on the wagon train looking at our girl. We want to get to the ranch without some guy trying to claim her."

Mid morning sunshine cast a silver shine on the hair of the older lady and touched with a warm gold glow on the dark red/brown hair of the two young women. Their brown eyes with gold glints, were sparkling with interest.

James with Tom, Tom's wife, Rosalea and their daughter Dawn, were sitting around the table in the home of Rosalea's parents, John and Mary Bjorson.

"I remember, as a small boy, I dreamed of going west," the older man injected into the conversation. "Even back then people were thinking of going west. 'Go West, young man,' was a saying going around." He had been quietly listening to the enthusiastic conversation.

"Really, Granddad!" Dawn exclaimed. "What happened? Why didn't you go."

"As time went by the dream faded before the necessities and changes of the realities of life. I became a Doctor, you know. I married your Grand Mother. Then your Mother came. I have been busy here in this community. Too busy for dreams."

"Come with us, Dad, you and Mother Bjorson." Tom Larson said. "I am sure that Rosalea and Dawn will be happier leaving here by having our whole family going west together. It would be good to have you go with us."

A quiet, "Yes," from the young woman. Were there tears in the back of her throat that sounded in her voice?

"Oh, yes!" from Dawn, "Please come with us, Grand Dad, Grand Mom! We don't want to leave you here. Be a doctor out west should be exciting and a really good thing."

"Having a Doctor along on the trip would be a good thing," James added. "And in the west, a Doctor will insure the settlement of communities."

They had been urged in other discussions for the trip. Now again, more urgently, the plea. The looks between the older couple spoke words, unspoken.

"We will wait until you get settled and then if there is a place for a Doctor, we will come." A smile quickly lit up the face of the Grandmother but faded into a slight frown.

"There will always be a place for you both, even if there are other doctors," Tom reassured him. "We will always need you, for your wisdom, as well as your loving companionship."

CHAPTER 2

The discussions and planning had been going on for the past weeks. James, the younger of the two brothers, had been 'West' for several years.

James had been 20 when the restlessness had led him to west. A restlessness that had made him want to see the wild country that was talked about. John Obey, a friend from the home town, was hearing the same talk and he decided to go too. Joining together they had gone west. They rode the train to the end of the track and joined a wagon train, working as a drivers for a freighter hauling much needed freight to the far west. They worked for the freighters going back and forth several trips each year. They went home and spent the winters at home, returning west with the first freight wagons going west each year.

One year, towards the end of the season, James and John Obey, had arranged with the freighters to ride with them part way to a place in the west, just east of the Rocky Mountains. A place that they had liked the looks of with the vast grass covered prairie. The Rock Mountains were the mountains off to the north/west. They hoped to find land for their ranch with a view of those mountains in the distance. James and John had each bought two horses and added a few things to their outfits and dropped off from the freighters along the trail.

They were going to see this land, look it over for a few weeks maybe. They had visions of many cattle and horses roaming the vast range. Days went by and they continued to travel on north to see more of the beautiful country. There were deer and antelope in abundance and back closer to the mountains they seen elk. One day down in a boggy lake area, they seen several moose! They were surprised as it was not known for moose to be south out of Canada.

They had wondered on toward the north sweeping back and forth from east to west as they looked over that land. One day looking back to the south, guessed that they were probably close to a hundred miles north of the wagon trail to California. Maybe farther than that, they thought, they had ridden many miles for many days. Never hurrying but looking at the country and the possibilities there. That afternoon they found another trail. A trail made by wagons, the trail leading westward. There was a stream near the trail. Although it was early, they decided to spend the night there at the stream. They wondered at that trail. It had been used with wagons some time before, but not much this year. They hobbled the horses and turned them loose. With water close and the grass was green and lush, it would be a good place to rest the horses and let them feed for a couple of days.

They had seen deer near at hand and stalked a nice buck down into a canyon not far away and killed one to have fresh meat. Knowing that it was too much meat to eat it all, and although they didn't really know how, they decided to try to dry some for later use. They cut thin strips and hung them on sticks near by.

Two days later, in the afternoon they could see wagons coming. It was a wagon train of about 2 dozen freighter wagons. The wagon train would be spending the night. In talking with the wagon train master, they were told that this was the trail to the new Oregon territory. They were returning east after the last trip west from this season. They were invited and urged to join them and go on east before the winter hit. They had refused, saying that they would be staying yet a while to look over the country before returning east to join their families. James told them that they had heard that there was a ranch that they wanted to find yet too. In the morning as the wagons headed east, John and James wished them God's blessings and watched them go.

Turning back to the north, and after traveling some distance, and as they often did when coming to a rise, they stopped to look over the scene before them. To their amazement there were cattle, great herds of them! They sat looking at all of the cattle. Groups and single dark red dots covered the prairie. Then they could see some riders.

"This must be the ranch we have been looking for," John said.

"Hello," they shouted as they took off to meet up with the riders.

Waving their hats, they galloped down to join them. They introduced them selves and they were asked if they were looking for work.

"The boss, Joe Ames, will put you on, we sure could use another hand or two. Come on, we are headed for the ranch." James and John were hired almost before they could get off from the horses. Two years they had worked for the rancher, learning many things in caring for cattle. They learned what hard riding and ranch work was. They learned to ride bucking horses and branding cattle and docking and dehorning calves was work needing done. They fell dead trees and hauled them in for fuel for heat and cooking, stockpiling enough wood for the long cold winter. They built muscles chopping the wood. They fell trees, cutting them into logs, and helped to build a long lean to on the back of the house and another on the bunkhouse to pile the wood out of the weather. They learned to cook for the crew, to work with and enjoy the company of the different men. There were a couple of older men but most were young. They all appeared to be honest, hard working men.

The riding was hard and their horses were turned out with the others to rest for a day or two. So each morning as they picked out a horse, they might get one that would buck for a few moments before it settled down to obey. But they found that the horses were good, hard workers.

One morning as James threw his lariat over a likely looking, line/back buckskin horse, one of the Ames sons, Blair, said:

"Not that one, James. Let me have him. He's tough. We haven't broke him yet. I'll try him this morning."

Hand over hand up the rope Blair walked to the horse. Snubbing him to the snubbing post. Blair talked to him and slowly put the saddle blanket on, then the saddle. The horse snorted and reared throwing off the saddle and blanket. Blair repeated the process a few times and finally got the saddle cinched on. Then the bridle. That was a fight. Finally, with the bridle on, Blair pulled the horse's head down and he grabbed the ear in his teeth and leaped into the saddle. Releasing the ear, "Open the gate," he yelled. The horse reared, then headed through the gate, bucking. Out in the open, the horse bucked wildly, snorting and screaming. Blair was thrown high but hung to the reigns and catching the main, leaped into the saddle. Again he was thrown and the horse, biting at him, he struck at Blair with his front feet, Blair dodged but the horse managed to strike Blair's right leg. Then again, the horse tried to bite him. Blair punched the horse on the nose, grabbed the mane and leaped into the saddle. Blair yelled at the top of his lungs and raked the horse with his spurs, shoulders to flank, again and again. He slapped the end of the reigns as hard as he could across the shoulders and on to the flanks. The horse plunged, twisted and turned as he bucked. Finally the jumps were less and less and he came to a stand still, head down, breathing with gasps, mouth open, nostrils flared. He stood spraddled legs, trembling.

The men had watched and then began to shout and cheer.

When Blair stepped off of the horse, they could see blood running out of the top of his boot.

Joe Ames, seeing the blood, said "Blair, go let your Mom help you bind up that leg."

Joe Ames picked up the reins and led the horse into a stall in the barn. The horse, head down followed. One of his sons helped him to rub the animal down. They left it in the stall.

James said, "Thank God that I didn't try to get on him!"

"Ya, me too! That was some ride!" John agreed.

John and James got thrown a few times but soon were able to handle most of the horses without getting bucked off very often.

The first winter was very cold and the work harder than ever until the cattle worked down into the bottom of a canyon where there was shelter and little snow with plenty of feed. They spent a couple of weeks with the cattle down in that sheltered area. One day the boss himself came down to double check on them, he told them that the cattle were sheltered enough with plenty of feed, that they didn't have to stay with them.

Back at the ranch, there were little chores during the winter. Splitting wood and keeping fires going was mostly what they had to do. The evenings, gathered around the fire, was a pleasant time. Story telling took up a large time in the long evenings. Stories that soon proved to be tall tales, each one trying to out tell the others' tales. Much laughter and jollying each other followed.

On a Sunday, they were invited to the ranch house to eat dinner and supper. Joe Ames took up a big old Bible and read from it while they sat around the fire. Joe Ames and his wife, Beth, talked about the Bible and some of their experiences out there in the wilderness when they relied on prayer to see them through.

"I soon discovered that to pray first was the way to do, when something happened." Joe Ames continued, "We were alone here and no one for many miles, days or weeks away. Many times in the wintertime I wondered why I ever brought Beth out here, and vowed that in the spring, I would take her out. Then spring came and a baby came and we were too busy to go. Beth would remind me that we were trusting God, so we prayed. When the first baby came, I was nearly scared to death, but Beth was calm and helped me through it." He stopped and sat looking at the fire.

Blair said, "Dad, you said that Mom helped YOU through it!" He burst out laughing. "Mom helped you through it," he repeated still laughing.

"Yes, we were all alone here. There wasn't any women or anyone else here. I had to help her. All by myself!" It slowly dawned on how it must have sounded and he broke out laughing too. Slowly the rest started to laugh, family and riders.

Megan went over and sat on his lap. "Well, Dad, by the time I, the youngest came along, how did you manage? Or did your daughters cause you as much trouble as the boys?"

Ames laughed and rumpled her hair, "To be honest, it scared the spit out of me when Connie came. When you came, it wasn't quite so bad. I had survived a little better with each one after Blair, with Ben, Matt, Wyeth and Caleb, and Connie before you came."

"Mom, were you ever afraid that Dad might not make it?" Megan asked. She was still laughing.

"Well, he really didn't know how tough he was yet. We were just kids ourselves yet then. We were on a wagon train that was headed for California. Joe's mother had died and his Dad had sold everything and headed west. His Dad was killed when he was helping another wagon put a new wheel on. That left all of the three wagons of their stuff to Joe. I think that he needed me. He asked me to marry him, but my Dad said no. We snuck off and had a preacher marry us without any one knowing. Then in the morning Joe tied the horses with the wagons together and the train had started to move out before he could get his outfit to going and he was a ways behind. I was walking and picking flowers to take to different women. No one noticed that I was gone. I ran back to Joe and we headed off to the north. A rain storm hit and hid the wagon tracks and we hid in some trees. I don't know if anyone ever went back to look for us. We kept on going north for a while and here is where we stopped."

"How come you never told us all that before," Blair asked. "Dad, you should have told us,"

"You don't tell things like this to little kids and by the time you were older, it just had become part of our past," Ames said.

"One thing about it, it sure beats all of the tall tales we have been telling out in the bunkhouse," Matt laughed.

"That's for sure," several agreed.

Joe Ames continued, "With the three wagons and the supplies we had, we only had to kill a deer or an elk now and then. I still had money and in a couple of years, I went out and brought in a few cattle and brought back a wagon loaded with some salt, flour and some potatoes and garden seed. We have done pretty well."

"Indeed we have," Beth said. "And look at our family, and all our riders. You are a good bunch of hands, and we thank you for your loyalty and hard work."

Connie and Megan brought a large spice cake and served it with a fresh pot of coffee. Many Sundays were spent with the riders in the ranch house but never one quite like this one.

CHAPTER 3

The winter gave way to spring with the melting snow and John and James, they with the Ames crew, went down into the canyon and found newborn calves. There were long days riding and watching out for the calves. They carried rifles on their saddles because there were coyotes harassing and taking a calf now and then, and occasionally a wolf. But the wolves becoming wary of being shot at, soon moved back into the high cliffs.

The men spent weeks hazing the cattle up out of the canyon bottoms and out to the open prairie where the feed was good and new grass coming.

One day they found some men that had killed a half grown steer. The boss, Joe Ames, told them that 'Hoss and cattle thieves' were to be promptly hung. They were 4 young men, and a boy of about 9 years old. When questioned they told that they had run out of food and hadn't found game so they killed the calf. When asked about the boy, they explained that they had found a burned out wagon. A small boy was hiding in the brush and that they took him with them.

"Why did you keep him?" Ames asked.

"Couldn't leave him there to die. His folks had been dead for a couple of days. We buried them and took what little we could find of the things for the boy."

"Where was all this?"

"Over north and east, up towards Canada. Looked like Indians work but most likely thieves. The wagons had been looted and the horses taken."

"How long ago?"

"Couple a years. In the winter we went down south a ways. Got work on a ranch. Worked at a couple a places. But most places don't need us all. We are brothers and we stick together. And most places didn't want the boy."

"And you are treating the boy like a brother."

"Been with us most long enough to be a brother," the youngest brother, not much older, said.

"Men," Joe Ames said, "If you men want work and work like the rest of the men, I will hire you on. Be honest and do the work. The steer that you killed, you are welcome to it. The boy can stay with the cook and help him until he is big enough to ride. There is plenty of work for the whole bunch. Shake my hand on it?"

"Yes Sir! I like that, we sure will!" The oldest, said.

"We are the Black brothers, from Oklahoma a few years ago. I am Blake Bart, Ben, Brand. And Chris," he introduced each in turn.

"Yes Sir, I will work for you," from each in turn as they shook hands.

"Me too?" the boy came with his hand outstretched too.

"Yes, you too," Ames grinned at him, shaking his hand.

"I am Chris Black now," the young lad said, grinning.

In spite of the hardness of the work, James and John enjoyed the life out on the prairie. Those years of hard work had paid off, and in taking most of their wages in cattle, they were accumulating a small herd.

They continued to ride with the Ames outfit, going in the fall, taking the steers to sell, and it was quite a ways. By selling their few steers, they were able to buy young more cows and the needed bull. Stock to build the herd.

Another year had passed, and again, they had taken the steers to sell and James and John had bought a few more young cows and another bull. As they were ready to leave to return to the ranch, they were approached by an older man and a young lad.

"Could you use a cook and a young hand?" The man asked. "I have a good chuck wagon," the man added.

"I quit the outfit that I came with. We found this lad along the way and they didn't want him and wanted to leave him. I have kept him with me. They were not a good outfit. I won't work for them any more."

James and John looked at each other, then grinned.

"We sure could use you both," James said.

"You are hired," John added, reaching out his hand. "I am John Obey, and this feller is James Larson."

"Wahll, my handle is Rock, just Rock. And this is Danny, he thinks that his name is Brock, so we sound alike.

"Danny is a good name and he lives up to it."

"Welcome to our crew," James said. "Are you ready to travel?"

"Well, we could use a few supplies."

James handed him some money, "Get what we need and meet us out by the cattle." James started away, turned back, "Here, buy flour, salt, lard and spuds to last us a year if you can. And anything and everything you can think of. As long as the money holds out, use it." He handed Rock more money.

"You want me to spend all of this money?"

"Sure, we can use the supplies. I hadn't thought of it. Good thing you came along."

John came, "Here, take this too. Maybe canned goods, Peaches is one of my favorites. Fill up the wagon. And buy any clothing and boots both of you need. Warm clothes. Plenty of them, with winter gear too. Get extra to last a year. Bigger sizes for the growing lad. Blankets, pillows, what you need. It can get cold where we live. We don't have anywhere else to get to buy things so get everything here."

The man stood there, looking at first one then the other of the men. He face showed surprise, then broke out with a big grin.

"C' mon Danny. Looks like we tied up with the right fellers this time!"

James added a saddle to the purchases and picked out a horse from the remuda and saddled it.

"Danny, here is a horse for you to ride. We could use your help with the cows on the way."

Danny's grin was something to see!

"When you get tired, tie him on behind the wagon and ride part of the time."

They were soon on the way to the ranch.

James suggested that the Ames crew go ahead on home, to not have to go as slow as they did because of the cows they were taking. He said that the three of them with the cook could manage. But two of the others stayed with them. The Ames crew took their chuck wagon on with them. While it was an uneventful trip back to the ranch, Rock and the chuck wagon and evenings around a campfire was enjoyed. The young lad was game but was rolled into his bedroll when he fell asleep at the fire.

John and James continued to help on the Ames ranch, early spring and through branding and the trip out to sell steers.

Then, lonely hard work building ranch homes on land the old rancher urged them to take up, hoping to keep them as his closest neighbors.

The rangeland was lush with grass and the vast area was large enough to have more than one big ranch. John Obey and James Larson, would be partners and had decided to build log houses close together, for their families.

They fell trees and cut them into logs, selecting near sizes, drug them in to where they wanted to build the houses and stacked them to dry for a while. From time to time, they fell trees and drug them in. Another year and with the dry logs they started to build the houses. They built houses big and solid enough to be comfortable to live in through the stormy, cold winters. Finally they had them ready for the roofs. Joe Ames came with a keg of nails. "Thought you fellers could use these."

"Nails! WOOPEEE, shouted James. John stood grinning widely, from ear to ear.

"You won't be needing these? I can order some but don't know how soon they will come. Next year most likely," James said.

"Nope, won't need these. I have another keg. Guess that I got carried away when I ordered nails. You are welcome to them. If you need more, come on over for some more."

"You are a life saver, Joe. Thank you. We were just wondering how we were going to put the roof on."

John wanted to build more on his house, making it bigger. James' house needed another room too, but was larger and nearly finished. They would live there until the families would come. They kept saddles and bridles there too, protecting and keeping them dry, always ready to use. After Rock and Danny came they all continued to live in the larger house. A bunkhouse would be built later.

Always working together, they built outbuildings, barns and a loafing shelter, all of logs. They built corrals with poles and a small pasture near by. It was to be partnership ranch. The friendship was as strong as family.

The accumulated herd of cattle was doing well, with plans to continue to increase the herd each year. The surrounding prairie would support many cattle. They could see that the possibility of large herds of cattle could happen with hard work and time. They planed to have a herd of horses too.

CHAPTER 4

They, John Obey and James Larson, had been gone away from home for several years and would go east to bring families back to the ranch in the west.

Before they left, they stockpiled plenty of wood to last a couple of years for Rock and Danny just in case, they didn't get back the next year.

From having worked with the freighters, John and James knew about when the last freighters would be returning east. They would go and camp near the trail and wait for the freighters and ride east with them and continue on to their families.

"We may have to wait for a week or more to catch the freighters, so we will go to the trail and wait," James said.

It was only three days before the freighters came by. Rock and Danny would return to the ranch taking all of the horses. They would spend the winter and be at the ranch when John and James returned, hopefully, the next summer. John and James' plans were to head west as early as they could leave the next spring to return to the ranch before winter should catch them. It would be too late now to return before the winter season came.

John's plan was to bring his family, his wife and two sons, to the ranch. James to encourage his brother Tom, to sell property left by their parents, and bring his family and join him in ranching in the west.

Tom had readily agreed and said that they would be able to increase the size of the herd of cattle with the money from the sale of the property. The winter was past and the sales completed, plans had developed into finalizing preparations for moving the families to the west.

Tom had continued to run the lumber/ yard and saw mill, after the death of his father several years ago. Tom and James had decided to take some building materials with them, materials to make the house more comfortable. James had helped during the winter and they had cut what they wanted to take with them and had stockpiled more lumber.

The sawmill, the lumber yard and the house had now been sold. The time was set to go. There were three large sturdily built wagons. One to haul lumber, windows and building supplies and equipment, the wagon was fully loaded.

They were nearly ready to go now, to start as soon as possible, hoping to catch one of the first wagon trains going west. The trip west would be accomplished during the best of the weather the spring and summer season. Planning to reach the ranch many miles to the north/west before an early snow might come and catch them on the trail or to be unprepared for the winter yet at the ranch. James hoped the first wagon train might be small and could travel faster. It was a long ways.

They were taking more than the recommended amounts so the wagons were all loaded carefully balancing and distribute weight, with stoves, a plow, farming implements of a mower and rake. A corn sheller and a small grinder to grind grain were put in the load.

Stoves were loaded on the wagon but no other furniture would go. Pots and pans, a dutch oven for baking, a large coffee pot and tin ware of cups and plates with forks, spoons and knives packed for daily use. The good dishes were packed in a barrel with towels and lots of other cloth padding them to protect them on the rough trip.

They remembered the coffee grinder when they put in the 3, 20 pound bags of coffee beans and it was added to the load. And garden seeds, other supplies wherever they could be packed in. The other wagon was for household goods, food, clothing and bedding with space for the two women to sleep. That wagon too, was packed high. They had talked about a small tent but decided against it. The men would sleep out on the ground or under the wagons. All of the wagons were heavily loaded, nearly ready to go.

James and Tom stood looking at the loaded wagons; "James, I think that we need to take Oats and wheat as well as corn for winter feed. We won't be able to harvest oats and wheat, unless we thrash it by hand out west. We will have no harvesting equipment."

"You are right," James said. "It will be too late this year to plant anyway. Next year we may try to plant some. We will really need to have the grain. How are we going to haul any thing more?"

"I don't know, unless we buy a couple of smaller wagons and hook them on behind the bigger wagons. Could we fasten them on behind the wagons that you and I will be driving?" Tom asked.

James: "I think that we could. We could try. But, let's buy a couple more teams and tie the smaller wagon on behind our big wagons. That way, we could unhook them and drive them if we need to. I have seen that done some times on the wagon trains. What do you think?"

"That sounds like the best way," Tom agreed.

They found two wagons not quite as big as the other wagons and filled them with bags of the grains and added several more bags of potatoes, tucking tarps safely over each wagon. They had to go out into the country to find two more teams of horses to buy. Now they felt that they would be well equipped and were ready to start.

They had talked to John Obey, and knowing there would be the need of the grain, he followed their idea and did the same, planning to hitch one wagon behind his wagon and one behind Jereme's, both loaded with the grain and potatoes. They distributed the loads between the wagons, balancing weight of the loads.

Earlier they had purchased teams of horses to pull the big wagons. James had horses on the ranch but they bought riding horses for each of them, mares and a Stallion for increasing the herd of horses. The Stallion, although he was very tame, would need to be watched that he would not cause trouble on the trip. Sometimes he would be tied and lead behind one of the wagons. The draft horses would be used for tilling, planting and other hard work on the ranch. All of the horses were tame and had been used to being with people. Children had been riding on them, just for fun.

The loaded wagons would all be put on a train to go as far as the end of the train tracks at Independence, Missouri. A passenger car on the same train would carry them and their bags of personal items. The horse drawn wagons, hauling the lumber and all, would complete the trip on west to the ranch.

"There will be wagon trains forming up at the end of the track. There will be wagons hauling freight and other ranchers and homesteader's wagons going on west too," James said. "We will join and be part of a wagon train."

John Obeys family were joining them, going west on the same train. John Obey, having returned for his family, had completed selling out and almost ready to go west. John Obey decided to follow James and Tom's plan of taking lumber and windows, building supplies for their ranch home out in the west. One of their wagons to haul those building supplies.

The Obeys, John and Lilly Obey had two sons, Josh and Jereme, who were old enough, and big enough, to help drive their three wagons. James and Tom had laughingly wished that they had a couple of boys to help. Maybe they could hire a man or two.

"I can drive," Rosalea said. "Dawn and I can drive a wagon."

"Yes," Dawn agreed, "Don't hire anyone to drive for us, Mom and I will drive our wagon."

"Yes, Tom, I think that Rosalea and Dawn can drive. You and I will be close," James agreed.

"We will hitch up the horses to a wagon and you girls can drive them around a few times before we load everything on the train," Tom said.

"Oh good," Dawn exclaimed.

"Yes," Rosalea agreed. "That will help. It would be good to get used to the wagons here at home and be ready to start on the trail west."

"Mom and I have driven the buggy around town but I'm sure the big wagons are a lot different."

"Handling the horses is much the same, but the heavy wagons will be different from the buggies. But you should be able to do it," Tom agreed.

"Maybe we should dress you up like boys," Tom laughed.

"I think that is a good idea. How about it, girls, would you wear men's clothes? James asked. "I haven't seen women wearing men's clothing around here but on the trip it would be good. Many women riding horses wear men's cloths and boots out west."

"Ab so lute ly! cried Dawn. "I think that I would like that. It would be fun."

"I think that would be a good thing for us to do, especially climbing in and out of wagons, walking around in the grass. And we will be helping with the horses too. Cumbersome skirts could be a problem," Rosalea agreed. "Pants and boots should be a lot easier for us."

"I think that you will be riding a lot out on the ranch, so the boots and boy clothes will be used a lot," James said.

"You will see out west on our range the grass land is the best that I have seen. The animals get fat out there, making it worth the cold weather of the winters. There are lots of sunshiny days, year around. The winter sometimes can be very cold with a severe snowstorm. Then it may warm up and be beautiful weather for a while before it turns cold again. Although the sun shines most of the time out there, we must be prepared for all kinds of weather. We must take plenty of warm clothes. I think that you girls wearing boys cloths would be best," James had continued. "Even on the ranch in the winter time."

"Yes," agreed Tom. "Safety and health are very important. Beauty can come after we are safely at home on the ranch. Then you can wear dresses when you want to. Not that you won't look good in boots and overalls. Let's take extras of everything."

"That would be best. Freight hauled out there will be costly and may not have what we would want. And nothing will go west during the winter. Maybe have to order something and not get it for months or even a year," James said.

"I already checked, there are no cowboy boots or big brimmed hats here. We will buy them in Independence," James added.

Thus the final shopping was spent, outfitting each one with plenty of warm clothing for the future, adding extra of foot wear, coats, woolen underwear and other clothing, extra of the warm bedding and canvas tarpaulins. Enough of extras to provide for several years. Rosalea and Dawn decided to buy Yarn and fabric of several kinds for making clothing and even curtains for the new house. A treadle sewing machine was safely stuck in somewhere. They would be well equipped in the new home.

Tom knew that the goods bought had made a big dint into the money from the sale and spoke of it to James.

"We have only a few hundred left to buy cattle," Tom said.

"Well, we will only buy a few cows at a time. And we will be selling a few steers each year. We can use the sale of the steers for the cows and not use the money. We can save the money for things we will need later. It will only take a few years until our herd will be multiplying pretty rapidly."

"That sounds good." Tom's concern for the money was satisfied.

One day her mother and father brought over a spinning wheel.

"Rosalea, this was your Grandmothers, and even I learned to use it," her mother said. "Maybe you should have a few sheep and spin your own yarn. I can show you in just a few minutes how to spin yarn," her mother told her.

"You mean that I can have this spinning wheel and take it?" Rosalea asked in surprise.

"Yes. It is yours now. Take it with you," Her mother said.

"Yes, by all means, take it with you, then I won't have to bring it with us when we come," her father said, grinning.

Rosalea threw her arms around them both, exclaiming happily at the gift of the treasured spinning wheel.

The wagons would have the protection of canvas covers, covered wagons, carrying the many needs to the new ranch home. The lumber and supplies, piled high on the wagon would also have canvas to protect the goods and the driver.

In the night, Rosalea had confided in Tom, the thoughts of possible dangers on the trip and the new life at the ranch.

"What if one of us should get hurt? I wish that my Dad and Mom would come with us."

"Yes, I too, wish that they would come. It would be a good thing, maybe for many people." Tom agreed. "A doctor will always be needed out there. There will be doctors going west too. But we know some things that will help. We have both helped your Dad and he taught us many things. We could set a broken arm or even a leg. Your Dad and Mom will come west soon. I know that it is a big move to go so far away, but I believe that it is time for us to go now. To have a better life in the new country. Living out there, on a ranch, with the cattle and horses. I am looking forward to it. Can you just think! James has described it. Out where there is so much open space. Where we can see for long distance, see beautiful mountains not to far off. To see our own cattle and horses running free, grazing on our own grass land. What a wonderful life it can be! We will be brave and make the move, right?"

"Yes. I will try to be brave. I think that it will be a much different way of life. I will believe that it will be a good new life," Rosalea said softly.

She smiled, "I am excited just thinking about it. But then I thought, out there so far from anyone, maybe we will get lonesome."

"We will be busy with much to do, and we will have each other. We are a family. And the Obeys are going to be there too. Oh, James said that he left a man and a young lad at the ranch too. That will be the 10 of us. Your parents will come soon, in a year or two. Do we need many others? James said that are two other ranches a few miles away that have families too. Maybe if it isn't too far maybe we can visit sometimes"

She felt somewhat reassured. She cuddled into his arms, her head nestled on his shoulder and went to sleep. Tom held her and silently prayed for protection and for God to watch over her and Dawn and keep them safe and well. It was some time before he slept. An apprehension came to him and he tried to put it out of his thoughts by praying.

"We will trust in God," he thought.

Rosalea spent a day with her father. Traveling in her fathers buggy, they visited several patients that day. One was an old lady that everyone called 'Aunt Meggy.' And young Milly McCarver, in her first pregnancy. Both had taken a fall and were slowly recovering.

"Dad, how could you leave now, regardless of you wanting to? Aunt Meggy needs you so. And little Milly. What if she lost her baby because of that fall. It was a sudden gust of wind that threw her down when she went to close the chickens in. They both need you. I can understand you not leaving here now, Dad. What a good man you are, a good doctor."

"Yet, how I wish that you were going with us. But I know how much you are needed here."

"Rosalea, I wrote a letter a while back, and got an answer today. A young man who wants to become a doctor is coming to work with me. He has been working with other doctors and will be a good doctor soon. In a year, maybe sooner, if he can take my place here, then I can come west to your country. This little town will be a good place for him to build his life's work." Her fathers voice was calm but had a bit of enthusiastic hope?

CHAPTER 5

Rosalea and Dawn spent time with the horses, talking to them, petting, brushing and grooming them. They spent time riding the saddle horses, then driving the teams hitched to the heavier wagon, gaining confidence each day. They were getting acquainted with the animals.

"Mother, they are all so beautiful!! Don't you think so?"

Dawn spoke quietly, reaching out, hugging and petting the copper neck of the horse that was her own to ride. The mare reached around, her nose touching Dawn's shoulder, as if wanting more attention.

Rosalea held the halter of the horse that was to be hers to ride. It too was a mare with a white coat and mane, rare in that country. The mare stood quiet, her ears pointed forward, her whole attention, great dark eyes looking at Rosalea's face. Rosalea's eyes traveled from the soft pink nose up to the eyes that were looking at her. Rosalea's hand followed her eyes, touching the cheek just by the eyes.

"They really are beautiful. Pearl is a real gem. I'm going to call her Pearl. What do you think of that, Pearl? Would you like that name, Pearl?"

She stepped closer, putting her arms around the neck. The horse made a soft whicker and shook her head up and down as if approving.

"This is Penny!! She is as bright as a new copper Penny!" Dawn voice bubbled with enthusiasm as she patted the neck of the horse.

"Have Dad and Uncle James named the other horses?" Dawn asked, as they went to the other horses. The stallion had been whickering and tossing his head every few minutes for some time.

"I don't know, we'll have to ask them," Rosalea laughed.

"Well, I am going to name them. This mare is Lady and this beautiful silver man is Silver King!" she reached out her hand towards him. The Stallion stepped to her, sniffing of her hand.

"Oh, you think that I should have a treat for you too," she reached in her pocket and pulled out an apple. "See here, I saved one for you too." He bit off a bite, leaving the rest in her hand until he took the rest. They had given apples to the mares.

"Silver King, you like apples, don't you! King, what do you think of that name. King. Do you have more apples Mama, we have this other girl to give an apple to too."

"There is more in the basket that we brought out, but here is one for Lady." Rosalea was holding the apple for the Palomino mare. Lady wickeder and nodded her head.

"What do you think of Lady for your name, hunh, Lady, you beautiful blond!"

"Lady! That is perfect for her," Dawn agreed, "Lady."

Then they went on to the big draft horses.

"We may as well name them too, whether the men like the names or not. The horses so far seem to like their names," Rosalea said. "How about Prince and Princess for these two, the pair of blacks."

"Good, and Duke and Duchess for the two Bays," Dawn said.

"And these two, who can they be? The sorrels? How about Sam and Suzy?" Rosalea wondered.

"And these Strawberry Roans? They just brought them yesterday," Roaslea asked.

"Strawberry Roans! How about Dolly and Billy Boy?" Dawn asked.

"Good names! Dolly and Billy Boy. That is just then names for them."

"Perfect!" Dawn exclaimed. We have them all named, now we just must always call them by their names so they will learn who they are when we call them."

Of the draft horses, Duke was a stallion. Prince and Sam and Billy Boy were big geldings.

"Won't that be great when they will come to their names!" Rosalea agreed.

Knowing that they would be with the horses every day was going to be a good time. They would enjoy the animals. They were admiring and beginning to love the animals. Even the heavier draft horses were responding to the attention and whickered greetings when the girls came near each day. They continued to call the names of each horse as they curried and brushed them when they spent time every day with them, repeating the name several times.

"I think that they know their names already. Don't you thinks so, Mom? Watch King. King," she called, "King—hello, King." He came hurrying to her, nodding his head and whickering softly. She laughed and petting him, talking to him before she gave him his apple.

"But we won't always have apples to give you. Maybe a hand full of grain?"

Rosalea and Dawn were looking forward to riding the horses and working with the horses and cattle. Yet wondering what and how they would learn all the things they would need to do. They talked about what it might be like in the new place, the ranch where they would live. They knew that they would have many new experiences. They also knew that there may be things that they wouldn't know and couldn't imagine and would need to learn to do, that the work could be hard.

CHAPTER 6

T he train cars had been sitting on the siding for days waiting for their possessions to be loaded. The week had sped by and the day came when, early in the morning, the last things and the horses were loaded on the train. The long dreaded goodbye's tearfully said, with prayers and blessings from the parents, they climbed into the passenger car and the train pulled away from their home. Leaving, perhaps forever.

With tear stained faces, Rosalea and Dawn sat amid bags for while, but soon moved things to be comfortable for traveling. Lilly Obey in tears too, sitting near by. The men had stayed in the car with the horses, to calm them. The Obey boys, Josh and Jereme, spent the day in the car with the women. The young people soon became interested in the passing terrain, rivers, farms with animals. Exclaiming over many things. Surprised at the different towns.

The sadness of separation from home and loved ones lingered, but it was being replaced with the interest and excited anticipation of the new life to come.

In the dark night, for many nights, thoughts of home/bound loved ones crept into their thoughts and prayers.

"Look at the differences in the way of life for other people, even here in civilization." They were passing through a larger town with larger houses, most painted white with white fences. There were bigger stores and other large buildings.

"Look at that Church!"

"Look at the steeple!"

Many were the exclamations over the different sites.

"What will it be like out in the West away from all this?" Josh asked. "There won't be big buildings or even like in our town."

"I guess that we will find out when we get there," his Mother answered. "Your Dad has told about many things. He said that he built our 'cabin,' he called it, out of logs. Some day we may build a bigger house out of rocks or logs."

"Yes, I am sure it will be very different. James has told us some about the west and the new home where we go," Rosalea said. "I think that I will like to have a log house."

"Me too," chimed in Dawn. "I wonder if we will have a rock fireplace."

"I think that James said that we will have a big stove. Anyway, we are taking our stoves, both heaters and cook stove. And James bought another cook stove too. He said that it was for the bunkhouse."

Rosalea continued, "He calls it Big Sky country. You can see for many miles, in all directions. That is hard to understand, but he says that it is so. Here we have hills and valleys and even mountains. But James says that our mountains here are just small piles of rocks and dirt, compared to the mountains out west. I am anxious to see it all. And it is a long ways between neighbors, and not many people living out there. No one next door. That will be very different from back here."

"We will have a new life. It will be just us and the Obeys," Dawn said. "I hope that I can learn to be a rancher and a cowgirl, and do good out there. I am excited. A bit scared, maybe. But I am determined to meet the challenge and do my best. How different it will be!"

The train trip was uneventful in spite of the wonders of the passing sights. The men and the young men were taking turns to care for the horses.

At the end of the track, the last of the goods were loaded on the wagons as the wagons were taken off from the train. James and Tom found a wagon master and he directed them to pull the wagons out to where two wagons were already parked.

Their wagons were well loaded. The women moved into the wagon and arranged it to be as comfortable as possible, ready to travel even though it may be days before the wagon train left. This would be their home for many weeks to come.

"Come on," James said as soon as the wagons were parked. "We are going to find Cowboy boots and hats."

Rosalea and Dawn were delighted with them.

"Should we buy two pear each?" Tom asked.

"That is sure a good idea," James answered. "My engineer boots that I was wearing when I went out were a terrible wreck before some came that the boss had ordered. And they were a wreck too when I left to come home. I bought another pair in Independence coming home. Two pairs of boots for 6 years wasn't enough. Hopefully we will be able to order things in a couple of years."

After James saying this, they decided to buy 4 pairs each. "Just in case we can't order them for quite a while. And the winters can be hard. We could easily need several pairs of boots in one winter."

They bought additional of boots, jackets, shirts and overalls and heavy sox, as well, outfitting each one with 4 complete sets.

"It looks like a lot of clothes but it will be better to have them and not need them, than to need them and not have them," Tom said.

Cooking was over campfires and would continue to be for many weeks to come. Bread started in the morning would be baked in covered dutch ovens each afternoon or evening for supper and use the next day. On some mornings pancakes were made and relished. The thought about syrup, sent the women to a store for maple flavoring and more maple syrup, a whole case was available and they bought it. They bought another barrel of sugar. More salt was added to the supplies too. They bought a barrel full of bacon to add to their supplies, barrels that would be tied to travel on the outside on the wagons.

The cooking would continue to be much the same for the weeks to come, all the way across the prairie to the new home near the mountains in the Big Sky country!

Jess Logan, the wagon train master, came and introduced him self. He was checking out each wagon to be sure every one was properly equipped.

"Every thing seems to be good," he said. "The horses are some of the best, but your wagons are heavily loaded. I think that you need another team on each of the wagons. There is someone who have changed their minds and are going back so there are several animals for sale."

"Thank you Mr. Logan, we will go right now before they are sold," James said. "I should have known that after hauling freight."

They soon came back with the horses and milk cows that were for sale and each bought two. The cows would be tied and lead at the back of a wagon as they traveled. James went back and found a young milk breed bull to add to the milk herd. Covered cans for the milk were bought as well as buckets for milking. They, and the Obeys each bought some chickens, 4 hens and a rooster.

"Enough chickens to get a start, we can hope that they will set on eggs to hatch," Tom said of the chickens, "We can fasten the pens on the side of a wagon while we are traveling and set them down at night."

40

CHAPTER 7

The girls continued to pet and groom the horses, calling out their names and talking to them. Now they had to name 4 more. King got so that when he seen either Rosalea or Dawn coming he would wicker and come to them before they called his name, the others following. The men spent time with the horses and they were quite tame and responsive to them. Someone was with the horses watching them and they were moved around each day to feeding grounds near the camp.

Rosalea and Dawn did not yet don their boys costumes, but would when the wagon train moved out. None of the other women were wearing boys cloths yet either. Rosalea wondered if any of the women would don men's clothing. She was sure that many would not.

Many times Rosalea and Dawn milked the cows when the men were busy. They would have milk to share among the travelers. The horses and the cows required care and watching. There were many things for the men to do. Gathering wood for cooking fires fell to whoever could spend the time first. They gathered and stockpiled enough firewood to have enough for several days. Thus the way of life would continue for the months to come while traveling across the land. It would be a very different way of life for many and for the years to come.

Many evenings they all gathered around a camp/fire to get acquainted. Jess Logan often talking of the coming trip. But Logan could see that there might be a problem with two men named Dabbs. They were loud and their language not fit around women and young children. Privately he cautioned them but the talk didn't seem to take any effect

Both evenings and mornings were a busy time with the milking and taking care of feeding the chickens and the cooking of meals. The shared milk with others of the wagon train. There would be cream and some made into butter. Some days they found an egg or two that were added to the meal.

Their extra horses would join the remuda of other animals and be herded along the way. Many of the wagons had an extra horse or two. Tom and James would take their turns herding the remuda with Rosalea and Dawn to drive a wagon at those times. They hoped that there would always be the grass at the camping places as they traveled west.

There was a wait of another three days and the wagon train was forming as other wagons joined. James was impatient when three more days went by with no more wagons coming.

"Jess Logan, the wagon master isn't tough enough. The Dabbs are going to be a problem. They were here first and are claiming the first place in line. So Logan is letting the Dabbs wagons out in front but they should be in back. They don't get around until the rest of us are done with chores. They will make us getting a slow start every morning."

"What can we do? Can we help?" Tom asked.

"Not much, or we will be stuck doing their work for them." James sounded disgusted. "Maybe Logan will get tired of their ways and get them to do better."

James turned to Rosalea, Dawn and Lilly, "You girls stay away from the Dabbs. Do NOT ask them to eat, nor offer them food. Or you will have it to do the rest of the trip. If you and Lilly want to cook together, eat together, like we have been doing here, that will be good. We can share a fire, saving gathering of wood. It will go better for us all, looking out for each other, sharing chores. Our wagons are next to each other in line. I am glad that there are other good men next behind us. It looks like a good group on this wagon train.

"Will it be alright if Mary Stewe and her daughter, Susie Walls use our fire too? There is room at the fire so far," Rosalea asked.

"Yes, I would think so," James answered. "The men are good men too. It is good to have them next to us. Most of the people on the train are good people."

"How many wagons are there in the train?" Tom asked.

"Logan said that the last 6 wagons, makes 40."

"What about those wagons parked farther out? It looks like they are forming up too?"

"I asked Jess Logan and he said that they are waiting for a wagon master to come to take them on out on the trail to the Oregon Territory. I thought about waiting for them as the Oregon trail goes closer to our ranch, but it may be a week or maybe 2 weeks before they are ready to go. It is almost the middle of May now, it may take 5 months or more to make the trip. That will be into the last of August or first of September before we reach the ranch. I want us to start as soon as we can and it won't be far that we go alone after we leave this wagon train that goes on to California."

Tom agreed, "We will have things to do to get ready for winter. I just hope that the winter won't come early this year before we are ready."

One day Josh and Jereme were tossing a ball back and forth. When Dawn came and they tossed the ball to her too.

"Hey, you are pretty good with the ball,' Jereme told her, as she tossed it back. "Want to play?"

"Sure! Hey, there are several more young guys standing around. Go see, maybe we can have a ball game if you can get a few more to play with us."

Dawn put on her boys clothes and there was soon a spot marked out and a baseball game was being played. The noise of laughing and calling out in the game attracted attention and an audience surrounded them.

With others joining in, including some girls who begged to play. It turned out to be quite an exciting game, enjoyed by the players and audience.

Jess Logan, a few white hairs scattered in the temples, was a tall strong man of about 40. Many times he stood on a small rise, his sharp blue eyes thoughtfully over looking the wagon train. He was watching the people working around their wagons. Every day he would walk about among the wagons, talking to each one.

One morning, "Be ready to head out about 5 in the morning," Logan told each wagon. He stopped at the Dabbs' wagon and urged them to be ready to move out at daylight.

The next morning, standing tall in his saddle, Logan impatiently called "Let's move'm out." He waved his right arm in a circle and on to the west.

As the wagon train readied to move out, the drivers on their seats, taking up the reins. Logan finally took his long whip and cracked it over the Dabbs horses, first one team then the other, getting them started, the Dabbs, cursing, scrambling aboard their wagons. The horse drawn wagons soon were traveling at a good clip. The day went well, leaving the town and all signs of civilization behind, following an old trail, well traveled in years past. The trail heading westward was so far unused this year.

They nooned without water, which they had to do many times on the trip, but each wagon had water kegs or barrels of water hanging on the outside. Camp for the night was beside a small stream, a place where there was grass for the animals as well as the water. Each wagon had been advised to refill all water containers at every opportunity and to use the stream water for the need of the day. The night was a new experience for many, being out away from any buildings and people. It was quiet with only a gentle breeze whispering in the grass.

And so the trip was started and continued, with Logan having to start the Dabbs teams with his whip every morning. Some mornings Logan had to get the Dabbs out of bed to harness their horses, while the rest waited. The Dabbs complained that they had not fixed breakfast yet.

Regardless of Logan advising them, and rousing them each morning, the Dabbs continued to be a 'thorn in the flesh' of the wagon train, causing the rest to wait for them, sometimes for an hour. That shortened the days traveling time. One evening as the wagons were stopping for the night, Logan rode up and quietly spoke to James and Tom,

"Leave a little more room between your wagons and Dabbs' wagons. In the morning pull around them and head out. I will tell the others. Dabbs may find themselves left alone on the prairie."

The Dabbs were still asleep when the wagon train moved out the next morning. Night found the Dabbs come joining the camp while others were caring for the animals, and suppers nearly ready. The Dabbs camped at the rear of the train. The third night, the Dabbs pulled around and stopped in the front of the group, out of the circle but headed west, out in front again. Morning found them ready in time. Were there grins on faces that morning?

No one enjoyed the Dabbs' company. They were loud with bad language and cursing, regardless where they were, if there were women present or not.

The days running into weeks, the terrain different at times, sometimes rough, yet the traveling much the same. Monotonous at times. Sitting on the wagons for hours at a time, they grew tired and achy. The drivers sometimes tied the reins up and they walked beside the horses for a while.

One evening as they circled to camp, they could see heavy clouds off to the north/west. As they were finishing with supper and chores, a chilly breeze picked up and it began to spit snow. Exclamations were heard through out the camp. Tarps were tied over the wagons, covering the exposed seat areas. The horses and cattle were put inside the circled wagons and most of the men crawled under wagons rolled into canvas covered bed rolls. The snow pellets were heard for a while on the canvas covers, but the sound died and quiet reigned. They thought that it had continued to snow. Morning came and to every ones surprise, there was very little snow on the ground. The snow had stopped with the few pellets. It was cold and people stood near the fires while they ate. Breakfast over and the wagons were soon on the way.

Each morning, Lilly would cook breakfast while Rosalea and Dawn went out to where they could see the horses and they would call to King and he would come to them, the other horses following. They didn't need to ride out and drive the horses in like many of the others had to. Josh and Jereme were helping with all of the horses to feed, helping with teams to be harnessed, ready to go. By Dawn and Rosalea calling the horses' names, the horses responded by coming to them. They were often treated to a handful of grain. The girls and Josh and Jereme would help putting on harnesses. After they ate breakfast, the men with Josh and Jereme would finish getting the horses hooked up to the wagons. The women took care of milking the cows and the milk and would clean up and pack up after eating. They would all soon be ready to go. The mornings were quite busy all along the wagon train, everyone trying to be ready to go as soon as possible.

A few places along the trail there was a Fort, with solders. Some supplies could be bought there. But the Obey/Larson's did not need supplies and did not visit the forts.

For days the terrain had been rough and hilly with small streams crossing at intervals. One day as they came out of the river breaks onto more open prairie, the view was of more level land. The trail leading more west from north/west disappearing miles away over a slow rising of the terrain. The land was covered with last years growth of grass that had grown quite tall.

Jess Logan came by, "This is called 'Tall Grass Country."

Many were the exclamations of wonder and approval of the sight. The abundant grass was a welcome sight; the animals would have good grazing close to the wagons at night. No need to take the animals away from camp to find grass.

Bones were seen from time to time, and as they were eating supper that evening, Dawn asked about what the bones were.

James said, "The bones are from buffalo. There was a slaughter of buffalo and only the hides taken and shipped away to make hats and other things. It was a bad thing to do. The Indians used the buffalo for food, but only killed what they needed but they salvaged all edible parts. Even the hides and horns were used. They tanned the hides and used them for tents, Teepees and footwear and beds and robes. Depleting the buffalo has caused much trouble for the Indians."

"And all of those bones are from those killings? There are hundreds of them."

"Yes, that is true. It is a shame and such a waste. They are beautiful animals. There are a few far out west. And hopefully people will not kill anymore. Maybe the herds will grow again. I know that we will not kill any," James said.

As they progressed, wild flowers could be seen in the depths of the greening of the new grass that was almost a foot high down in the depths of the grass hay that was 4 to 6 feet tall.

From time to time Dawn jumped down from the wagon and picked a flower or two to bring to her mother, tucking it in her hair. "No wonder that they call it 'Tall grass country' it is taller than my head." But she found the flowers.

"Look Mama! See how beautiful!! And they are wild! God planted them!"

"The whole prairie is covered with them!" Rosalea said, her eyes sweeping the area along the trail and then out across the prairie.

"We are going to love the west! It has it's own beauty!" Dawn exclaimed.

"And the sky! The whole world is covered with a big dome of sky that is so incredibly blue!" Rosalea added.

The day was pleasant, the air warm with a little breeze from the north/west Although there wasn't much dust, the wagons spread apart some to let the dust settle between them. Everyone could enjoy the day. Much of the time, some of the people walked beside the wagons as they traveled. They were able to travel faster out on the more level and traveled farther those days.

They nooned again with water from the barrels, which they did many days. Although the stop was not long, the animals took advantage to eat of the tall grass and at times pushing aside the dry grass to seek out the green grass growing rapidly with the warm spring weather.

On Sundays, if it was a good spot to camp with water and good feed for the animals, they stayed there and had a good day of rest.

The days were getting longer and sometimes they came to the camping spot near water, early, before dark, be it stream or river. The longer evenings gave more time for the animals to rest and feed. The young people would get together and play ball again. There were shouts and laughter as the game progressed. With smiles on the faces of the others while they were busy about the camping chores. The trip was being enjoyed.

CHAPTER 8

Traveling on, one day they topped a higher rise looking into a valley where a small stream wondering along through low land. It was an ideal spot to camp and although it was early afternoon, Logan decided that they would stop for a couple of days and rest, letting the animals to feed at leisure. There was good cool water and good feed for the animals. The animals were quickly unhitched and turned loose to feed. The animals did not wander far from camp during the evening and night. Most of the campers took advantage of the warm days and the long evenings and with the clean running water for bathing, and some laundry. They hung the wet clothing over bushes and they dried in the warm sunshine.

The grass was abundant with many flowers scattered everywhere. Dawn ran about and picking flowers that she wove into a garland. She laughed, putting the flower rings on her mothers and her own head. She made one for Lilly Obey too. She made flower rings for the two women in the wagon behind them, a mother, Mary Stewe and her young married daughter, Susie Walls. They wore them all evening and when the men came for supper, the men laughed but admired the ladies fancy hair adornments.

Logan stood watching. "It is good to see the good fellowship among the group," he thought. "And the Logan's and Obey's at the center of it so much of the time. Good people!"

The night slowly came. The almost constant wind died to a gentle breeze. The supper over and all chores done, the men checking on the horses, Dawn and her Mother sat watching the moon rise.

"Look at that moon," Rosalea whispered. Even the animals had quieted, many lying down, replete from the thick green grass.

"It is so beautiful" Dawn's whispered answer.

The heavenly sky of indigo blue was lit with myriads of twinkling lights of scattered stars, while the rising round moon was shining it's self to utmost brilliance to sub/do the stars. They sat entranced at the beauty of the night.

Although the men were very quiet, the changing of the guards disturbed Rosalea and Dawn enough that at last they crawled into bed to sleep a peaceful sleep.

They continued to travel following up the stream as it flowed from the north/west. During the early evenings several of the lads and men caught fish and distributed them around the camp for supper.

A few days later the trail left the stream to head more westward. For days they were without water and again the water barrels were used until nearly dry. Eventually they came to a small river where they spent a couple of days allowing the animals to feed and rest. Laundry and bathing again, taking advantage of the water and time to get laundry dried again. Weeks at a time went by with out the luxury of bathing and laundry being done. And weeks of no wood for fires where, much to the discomfort of gathering buffalo chips for cooking fires, was the only way. The first time that they had to resort to the chips, some refused and had cold suppers. But their hunger overcame their dislike and fires were lit around camp.

Days went by with no water and water in the barrels was nearly depleted. The heat had become oppressively hot with no breeze. Jess Logan always on the lookout, seen a storm coming. He rode past the wagons and he yelled, "Big storm coming, circle the wagons, put the livestock inside the circle. Fasten everything down. Prepare for wind and rain!"

They were caught in the middle of the day with big clouds that brought wind with lightning and thunder and heavy rain.

They had put extra canvas over the front of the wagons when Lilly called to Rosalea, "let's catch the rain and fill the barrels."

They tied a canvas between the wagons making a deep trough to catch the rain and filled buckets as it filled the canvas. They opened the water barrels to let the rain help to fill them. All around the camp others did the same. All available containers were soon filled with the rain water.

The heavy rain continued. There were no fires and little supper that night, mostly of bread. The people stood around under stretched canvas for hours before they crawled into beds. The ground under the wagons was as wet as in the open. Those who slept under wagons finally rolled up under the canvas and slept on the front seats of the wagons, uncomfortable, only partly dry, sleeping fitfully.

The storm with heavy lashing rain lasted during the night. It was a large storm and finally the lightning part of the storm passed on to the east. The morning was still grey with showers coming off and on, and the sun didn't come out until nearly sunset. The prairie, even with the grass covering, had turned to mud, thick, slick, mucky mud.

They spent three days there before they were able to move on because of the mud. It was a dirty, miserable time for all. However, fires were started and food cooked. Wet and muddy clothing was washed using up much of the caught rainwater.

The washings dried in the warm sunshine. The weather, not as hot after the storm, was comfortably warm.

The animals spent the time feeding and resting during the forced stop.

The sun shining every day and when the train was able to move on again, they made good time across the nearly level land.

They had rains several other times, but none like this one. The rains most coming late in the day and they camped early and were delayed a few hours in the mornings. They crossed rivers and smaller streams, camping near water whenever they could. They came to country that was rough and slow going. For a few days they didn't make much distance, only a few miles each day.

They stopped a day now and again where there was good water and grass, and spent time letting the animals feed and rest and they were doing well, looking good. Washing clothes and taking baths were accomplished when ever possible.

One evening as they were stopping, Lilly came to Rosalea, "Young Susie Walls' baby is coming, we need to help her mom with Susie." The Obey lads helped Dawn with making the supper that evening. And the baby boy was born just before midnight.

Rosalea remembered that James had mentioned that sometimes a baby was born as the wagon train traveled. She smiled at that thought as she crawled carefully into bed, hoping to not waken Dawn sleeping near by.

They came again into rougher country, to a river with river breaks where the going was slower. The trail was a steep downward place to just before coming out to the flat bottom with the crossing of the river. The Dabbs' second wagon was stuck where a wheel broke turning down into the steep turning place.

The wagons had all slowed with the dangerous decent down to the river. The Obey's wagons were behind a ways, out of sight.

The rest of the train stretched out farther behind, each taking time to be careful in the decent to the river. Some were waiting for wagons to get far enough ahead that others could move a ways. James and Tom went to help the Dabbs with the broken down wagon. The Dabbs had a spare wheel but the wagon had to be jacked up to change the wheel. A rock was rolled in place and with a plank to use as a lever, Tom and James were trying to lift the wagon. But they had trouble raising the wagon because it sat leaning at a difficult angle. Tom took another plank and working in front of the broken wheel, James and Tom each levering to lift with a plank, were able to raise the wagon enough to free the wheel. The Dabbs were to take the broken wheel off and put the new one on while James and Tom held the wagon up. The broken wheel was off and the new wheel in being placed, did not go on immediately. One of the Dabbs let out a terrible loud curse. At the loud sound, the horses were frightened and leaping, lurched forward, throwing the lifting planks out. James was thrown against an outcropping of rocks and dirt. Tom was pinned beneath the wagon. Being behind the two wagons that James and Tom drove, Rosalea and Dawn could not see down over the bank. They set the break on the wagon and went to see what was happening. They got in sight just as the horses lurched and they seen Tom get caught under the wagon. The Dabbs just stood there. James, stunned by his fall, slowly got to his feet, shaking his head, his hand covered with blood from a cut on his head. Rosalea was kneeling beside Tom, calling his name, Dawn beside her. James, picking up the plank, yelled at the Dabbs, "come help me!" He put the plank on the rock and with the help of Dabbs lifted the wagon off from Tom.

"Pull him out," James called to Rosalea and Dawn. Her arms around Tom, she tried to lift him away. Logan was there and lifting Rosalea out of the way, Logan lifted Tom in his arms and carried him a few feet out of the way. Logan sat bracing and supporting Tom against his chest. Rosalea, Dawn and James knelt beside them.

"Tom!" her voice soft and low, Rosalea reached her hand to his face and turned his head a bit towards her.

"Rose, my dear Rose" his voice was low and hoarse. "Rosalea, promise me—that you will go on. Go on to—the ranch and make—a new life."

"We go together, my darling, my dear husband," she answered her hand gently against his cheek.

"Promise me,—Rosalea—promise—me—promise—me that —you—will—make—a—new—life—new—life—promise—"

"I promise, Tom. I promise," she reassured him.

"James,—James," his voice nearly gone, he turned looking for James.

"I'm here, Tom. Right here."

"James,—promise me—that you will—look out for Rosalea—and Dawn.—Take them—to the ranch—and—make a home—for them.—A—new—life—a—new—life."

"I promise, Tom, of course I will. You and they are my family, always have been and always will be."

"Rosalea,—promise—me—that you—will make—a—new life—on—the ranch." He seemed to rouse a bit with urgency. "a—new—life."

"I promise. You will always be with me there."

"That—may—not—be," blood was coming out of his mouth and his breathing was becoming more difficult.

"It is—beautiful—here on—the—prairie." His voice growing weaker—" I—stop here—here—I—stay—Jesus" his voice softly trailed off. He raised his eyes towards the sky, then slowly closed them. He had gone.

Logan continuing to hold him in his arms, they sat in stunned silence. It had happened so quickly! The Obeys and others coming to help if there was a problem, took charge and lifted them aside and onto the wagons. The Dabbs wagon was fixed and Logan ordered them to go on and clear the way for the rest of the wagons.

The wagon train circled and camped for the night on the other side, above the river. A grave was dug in a sheltered high place between some trees, overlooking the prairie and the river.

Logan sought James out to find out the truth of the accident. James, Rosalea, and Dawn were still in shock, anger had not set in yet, but Logan had recovered enough to go to the Dabbs,

"You are to take the very end back of the wagon train, stay out of the circle and under no condition are you to come near any of the Larson's or Obeys again," he told them. "And if I ever hear you or hear of you cursing or yelling again, you will leave the train behind us. You will never again travel another mile with us."

The night found Rosalea and Dawn huddled together, holding each other. "We must be brave and buck up, as your Dad would say," Rosalea told her daughter.

"I know, but, Mama—"

"I promised him. We must do this. We will go on and make the life in the west, a good life. Right now it is so hard, but he wanted to do this. He wanted to go to the ranch and make it a good place and a good life for us all. We must not fail in what he dreamed of, what he wanted to do, to have a new life out in the west. God will see us through."

"Yes, Mama, we will. God will help us. I don't understand why—"

"No we don't understand, but God will see us through what ever is to come if we trust Him. He will give us strength and courage."

"Please, Father God, help us "—was all that she could pray. The shock and the wound so sudden and deep. The loss was great and yet there could be no time to think about it. The wagon train must move on.

The next morning found Rosalea and Dawn helping James with hitching up the horses.

"I am driving Tom's wagon from now on," Rosalea said calmly, looking James levelly in the eye.

James studied her for a moment, "Yes, I know that you can do it. Dawn will drive the wagon she has been helping drive." He reached out and gave her a hug, turning to Dawn and drawing her into the hug too. Holding them he bent his head and prayed, "Father God, give us comfort at this time. Guide and lead us. Help us. Give us strength. Jesus, be our comfort and friend now. We ask it all in Jesus name. Amen." He had stammered and hesitated as he prayed, his voice sounding the tears that were choking his throat. How hard to pray at a time like this with his own heart broken for the loss of his brother. The loss was going to be very hard for them all.

The Obeys stood near by wanting to help, but not knowing how, bowed, joining in the prayer as James prayed.

"Well, we are ready," James called to Logan. Logan's face too was white and drawn.

"It is hard when I loose someone in the train in death," he thought. "And it was so unnecessary. Such a stupid thing to have happen. To loose a good man like Tom Larson. How can some men be so—so—" he couldn't find the words. The fact that Tom had died in his arms and he could do nothing to save him, was very hard for Jess Logan. Tears stung his eyes so that he could not see.

"Head 'em out!" called Logan hoarsely in a few minutes, waving his arm in a circle and waving them on to the west.

CHAPTER 9

There was a Fort near the trail and they spent a day there. Some supplies could be purchased by those who needed them. Letters were left at the Fort to be taken back east. But the wagon train left the next day.

Days dragged on into weeks as the wagon train moved across the rolling prairie, on towards the west. The routine became monotonous. People and animals tired. Days went by without water and again the barrels nearly dry and they cut rations. No washing of anything. Without water, the animals did not feed as much as they needed to.

Again Logan called a halt for a storm coming. They covered the open wagons and tied tarps to collect the rain water into barrels again. They immediately set out tubs filled with water to water the animals. Everyone collected water into every thing that would hold water. They left water in the tubs during the night for the animals to drink during the night whenever they wanted to. The storm was passed after a few hours, but the water barrels were full again. The next day they stayed there to rest and allow the animals to feed. And they left the water tubs out for the animals.

At times, they had passed trails that had lead off toward a Fort, some times to towns and settlements. But they had not come near a town for some time until one day when they came to a small town situated on a river, with trails leading off towards the North and South. The main trail continuing on westward.

"Evan's Junction" a weathered sign was painted on the largest building, beneath was a sign, 'Hotel,' hanging by one end. The wagon train camped near by the river. Several people wrote letters to be picked up by who ever were returning East.

Rosalea and Dawn had written from time to time, letters describing the country and events, waiting for this chance to mail them. They did not write about the accident. The wound was too raw to even write about yet. Several times a Pony Express rider had passed by going east and carried their letters home. Sometimes the Pony Express rider was going west.

A Pony Express rider stopped at the town, but came to the wagon train. He was looking for John Obey in Jess Logan's wagon train. There was a message for John Obey. John had urged and begged his father and mother to accompany them to the west. But they had hesitant at the thought of the great distance of the move, they had refused to go.

After John and family had left, his parents realizing the loss of the closeness of the only family that they had, changed their mind and had decided to come. They had hurriedly packed and joined another wagon train. His father had two wagons and the driver that he had hired had been hurt and was unable to drive. Could John come back and help them? The wagon train was about five days behind. The wagon train would continue on but it would cause difficulty for others who would help at times, but it could slow the train down by his father needing help with the two wagons. His Father had tied the second wagon to the back of the first wagon and sometimes it took time to get the second team to start.

By riding one horse and leading a second to trade off in riding, John with hard riding, could reach them in a couple of days or a little more.

Lily Obey would now drive a wagon. She was assured from watching Rosalea and Dawn, she knew that she could drive the wagon. Her sons were there, each driving a wagon. James was there if they needed other help. So John went to help his father and mother.

Over the years many pioneer women soon became brave and bold, heroic, doing what ever was needed, surpassing expectations, enduring hardships and trials. Many historic stories testify to the many brave pioneers that crossed the plains.

The Logan wagon train had no need for anything from the town and left the next morning. Much to the relief of many, the Dabbs did not continue with them. Jess Logan may have had something to do with the Dabbs not continuing with his train.

In another week they came to a dividing of the trail. One, the broader more traveled trail continued westward, bound for California. The other trail turned more to the north/west. They could see hills with a black look to the north. And farther to the west, although it was hazy, what looked like mountains.

They had spotted groups of Antelope from time to time and one or two were killed for fresh meat shared around the camp. The antelope were more plentiful as they went farther west. And they continued to see the big bones of buffalo and Dawn, tears running down her face, was deeply sad at the thought of the animals that had been needless slaughtered.

The next evening, indicating towards the hills to the north. "The Black Hills," James said, as they sat eating supper. "And the Tetton Mountains to the west. We are getting closer to home. Another week and we will be home."

In the morning as the Larson and Obey wagons prepared to separate to leave the wagon train, Jess Logan shook hands with each, then hugged the women, wishing them well and God speed on the remainder of their journey. Tears ran down his face as he turned away, remembering the loss of Tom Larson, the loss to the other members of Tom's family. Silently he prayed for them, that God would take care of them. He decided that when he quit leading the wagon trains, he would return here and go look them up. Maybe get a job on their ranch. Maybe he would become a rancher too. He decided that he would save every penny that he could. Jess Logan's wagon train, that was now six wagons smaller, headed for California, taking the trail leading off towards the west, a bit towards the south.

Six wagons with one man and two young lads quickly becoming men, with three women, each driving a wagon, would travel on alone, turning more toward the north/west. The extra horses were haltered and tied to the back of the wagons. With two milk cows each behind the other two wagons. The bull tied to the back of one of the smaller wagons. The chickens in their pens, still tied on the wagons, seemed to have done well. Each noon and night when they had stopped the chicken's pens had been put on the ground and the chickens fed and watered.

James, standing up on his wagon, looked back over his small group of wagons, felt a bit apprehensive at the responsibility, yet proud, proud of the bold women and lads driving the wagons. Dawn just behind him, Rosalea, then Lily. Josh Obey just behind Lily, Jereme, the oldest Obey boy, the last wagon. Six wagons, each with a driver! Six wagons in his little train with 4 more wagons with teams between, without drivers. James groaned at the possibility of a problem. He shook his head, "We will trust God to take us the rest of the way home to the ranch."

"In another week we should be at the ranch,—home," James reminded himself. He wondered how things were at the ranch. He had left an older man and a young orphaned lad that he had befriended, Rock and Danny, in charge, to watch over the cattle and horses. Well, what ever, if the cattle and horses were gone, the land would still be there. And the buildings and corrals, he hoped, and Rock and Danny safe and well.

Days passed while the terrain grew sandy and dry, sagebrush in abundance for miles before grass appeared again as they came into higher country. They continued to see groups of Antelope occasionally but James decided that he wouldn't take one as the weather was warm enough that part of it might spoil.

Everyone had grown weary from the long weeks, months of traveling. The nights didn't seem to be long enough, yet, the days didn't either. Still the days seemed interminably endless. Now alone, they missed the presence and attention that Jess Logan had had for them. Logan had spent time with each of the group of wagons. They missed Logan's quiet strength.

"We will be home to the ranch in a week," James tried to encourage that night as they sat at supper.

The next day they met a group of Indians traveling across from the west to the north/east. There were women and children in the group, horses pulling travois heavily laden. They looked to be moving some distance. There hadn't been word of trouble with Indians and James knew that the Natives wouldn't risk women and children. James stopped the wagons, got down from the wagon and motioned the leaders of the Indians to proceed. Three of the men came over and spoke to James. James greeted them the best he could. They spoke about the good day and good travel.

"We travel far west," James waved his hand to the north/west.

"We travel north," the man answered.

"You have families, children, small ones, it is good," James commented, smiling. The man nodded, looking back at the travelers.

"It is good," he answered and smiled, holding his hand up, then raising his hand in farewell, he turned back to the front of the column of travelers and rode on.

James stood and they watched the group move on a ways before they continued on their own journey.

As they traveled into the higher country, they came to a river wondering and circling around but running swiftly. Although the river was swift, it was not very deep, easily crossed. Fish were abundant in the river and the lads caught fish for supper each night. A welcome change. They followed near the wondering river but continued on north/west for a few days. The way lead steadily higher. The blue looking mountains off to the Northwest grew higher, yet seemed to stay aloof and far away. Then one day, there appeared to be white on the tops of the still far away peaks. There had been snow high up on the mountains.

"Another day and we will be home," James said as they sat at supper that evening.

"Tomorrow?" Dawn asked.

"Tomorrow, if we don't stop long at noon."

"Our ranch looks like this?" Rosalea asked, her hand waving at the area around them.

"Yes. And the river runs through our land and near the buildings is a smaller stream. That will be water for the house."

"The grass is nearly as high as my head!!" Dawn exclaimed.

"And it is like this everywhere?" Rosalea asked.

"Not every year, but most of the time," James answered.

"OOoooh!!!" from Dawn.

The mountains off to the west seemed to grow higher as they traveled towards them, yet they were still far away. The blue mist of distance grew more dim, with more details showing up.

There were more of the wild animals, both of the antelope and deer. All seeming to be more plentiful, and seen in larger groups. They seen buffalo, a small bunch at a distance, the first they had seen.

CHAPTER 10

L ater. "Smoke!!" Suddenly James could see a column of smoke as they topped over a hill. There were buildings about a mile away. The buildings were all built of logs but had good shingled roofs and doors and windows that had been hauled in.

"This wasn't here when I left," James thought. "Something new. I wonder—" The buildings were not far from the side of the trail. The trail branched off, one going on westward and a faint trail going to the north/west towards their new home.

James turned on towards the buildings and stopped. He jumped down off the wagon and came back to the others who were climbing down too.

"Our ranch is off this way north about 5 miles. The Ames' ranch about 20 miles off to the west," he waved his hand.

"Let's see what all we have here." James said. "This has all come since I left 9 months ago. Well!"

They walked over to a building with 'Culbert's General goods' painted on the front. The next building appeared to be a blacksmith shop with corrals and a barn behind. On the other side was a generous sized house with a wide covered porch. A sign hung from the porch roof, 'Molly Craft's Boarding House.'

'Bath and breakfast' painted underneath. There was another but smaller house and a small distance on, a larger building.

A man stood in front of the store, greeting them, "Welcome to Culbert's Corner. I am Will Culbert," extending his hand to James. James introducing himself and each of his group.

"I have heard of you. You own the ranch off to the north," Culbert said.

"Yes," James agreed. "We are just arriving home. This place, 'Culbert's Corner, is new since I left here. It looks like it is a good place for it, on the trail going west. It should be a help to travelers as well as to us ranchers."

"Yes, that is what we thought. We freighted in here last fall and built as best we could before the snow hit. We have continued to build and fix all spring and summer. We have good water here, and lots of it. Yes, the wagon trains will stop here. At leased the last one going east last fall did."

"Here comes my brother, Dan. He is the blacksmith. General repair man, among other things. Our sister, Molly Craft, her husband died and we brought her with us," he waved at the building, where she was coming out the door. "She cooks for us. Dan and I live in her house as long as she has rooms. When the rooms are full we have to bunk in the back of the store," he laughed. "But that will be only during the summer, if at all."

Other people came to welcome the travelers. There was a young man and wife, Jonathan and Saraha Brooks, "Minister and teacher," Jonathan said, introducing them selves.

Molly Craft came to welcome them.

Jonathan Brooks greeted them "Welcome home. It is so good to see you. Do you know if there are more wagon trains coming soon?"

"Yes, there is one coming about a week behind us. They are going on to Oregon," James assured them.

"We don't have a very large congregation or school students, Jonathan Brooks grinned. "But someday soon there may be more. Maybe some of the rancher's children will come and stay here with us and attend school. And when the wagon trains stop here for a day or two, we are here." He added, "There was a couple of weddings when the wagon train stopped here. I can do that, marry people," he grinned. "The winter was long with just the few of us here."

Will Culbert, pointed out to the south to a field, "With Dan's plow and all of us working, we are going to raise some grain and a garden. The garden will be our biggest asset." Will continued; "Our garden and grain will feed us, and we should have some that we may sell. The gardens are really growing, and doing well, so there are fresh vegetables and there will be a lot more and potatoes and beets soon. We will have quite a good supply of dried corn, beans and peas and many bushels of potatoes and beets to last the winter. All the rest of the summer and on into fall season with travelers getting here, I think that fresh vegetables will be greeted warmly."

"The season has been very good," Jonathan Brooks added. "Spring came early and then we had rain when it began to get dry. With warm weather, everything has really grown."

Molly Craft added, "We have chickens, and a few sheep. How about me selling you some of my sheep? The herd keeps on increasing, had a bunch of lambs this spring. I have wool for sale too."

"I just may buy a couple of your sheep. I have a spinning wheel," Rosalea answered.

"You have a spinning wheel? Mine fell off of the wagon and broke so badly, we couldn't fix it," Molly exclaimed.

"We will have to share!" Rosalea laughed.

"You are the first wagons to come this year," Culbert said. "And only one group of wagons last fall going east."

"Yes but like I said, there is a wagon train coming this way to go on to the Oregon territory. They are maybe a week behind us," James told him.

"The season is just started. It is a long ways across the land from Independence and it takes a long time to travel that distance. There will be many more people coming west, some going on to the Oregon Territory and some to California." James continued, "Every where we went back east, there was talk of moving west. It is like a fever, catching on. Itchy feet, there are those wanting to go exploring, just to see the new sights. Some have 'gold fever' too. Especially many young single men, they are going to come on west. There should be several wagon trains coming this summer yet. You may be busier than you will want to be."

"There are several wagons loaded with much needed supplies coming. I intend to stock many things, that is why we built such a big building to store it in." Culbert added, "I am expecting them coming soon. I thought maybe that was what was coming when I saw your wagons," Will Culbert said.

"One thing we wish we had been able to bring was hogs," James said. "How are we going to get along without bacon."

"I have ordered some hogs as well as bacon. Sure hope they come. I ordered a whole big wagon load of hogs. Don't know how many that will be. One bore and all of the sows they can put in. Hopefully they will be on with the next supply wagons. Do you want one or a couple of sows?"

"Yes, we sure will take one if you can spare them."

"We will see what we get."

"Well, it is good that you people are here and we will surely be back over soon, but we had better get going and get set some before dark," James said as he climbed up on the wagon.

Rosalea called, "We will be here for Sunday service." With waves, they headed for the ranch.

70

Five miles out they came to the ranch, John Obey's ranch house first.

"Here you are, Lilly Obey, here is your new home!"

"Oh!" tears were running down her face.

James lifted her down, Josh and Jereme joined them.

"Oh! Our new home! Josh, Jereme, look!" They stood looking around.

"This is really good, Mom! Better than I thought it would be!" Josh exclaimed.

"Yes!" was all that Jereme could find words to say.

"Can you manage or shall we stay for a while and help you?" James asked.

"We can manage," Josh said.

"Thank you, James for all,—everything. We can manage, and John will be home in a few days with his parents. We can do this. You go on to your house before night catches us." They could see the other house just a short distance away.

"Send one of the boys over if you need any help, but wait for John to get here to do much. We will be over to see you soon," James assured them.

Tears had came to Rosalea's eyes as she embraced the sight of the ranch buildings, the houses and the other buildings with the rolling grassland extending away. "It is beyond my greatest dreams," she whispered.

The ache returned to her heart at the memory of her lost husband and his dreams of the ranch.

"If only Tom could have lived! He would have loved it here. He had such hopes for living out here in 'God's country,' like James calls it. I believe that it is, is going to be. We will make it so. It may be hard, but we will have a good life here. Home! Home on this beautiful prairie! Home for Dawn as well. Will there be a good man for Dawn here? And soon, home for my Mom and Dad! Please, Father God, guard us. Guide us. Teach us that we may make this like the 'promised land,' fulfilling James' and Tom's dreams for us in this land." The tears stopped and peace came as they came the short distance on to the house.

James shout; "Home!" The ranch buildings and corrals at hand.

"Home!" "Home!" shouts from Rosalea and Dawn. The long trip was ended! They were home. He directed them to pull the wagons with the house hold goods and the lumber to be parked not far behind the house as he stopped the other wagons just on past.

They were greeted by an older partly crippled man, 'Rock', just 'Rock', he had said, and a young lad, Danny Brock, about 10 years old.

"Looks like you two have kept things in good shape," James greeted them.

"Yes, things have been good. The winter was open, not as cold as some can be in this country. Haven't lost a cow, nor a calf. Have a new foal."

"Good job, my friends."

"James, the Ames riders came and helped to doc and brand the steers this spring. They came a few days ago and took our steers to take with theirs to sell. I think that they are going to bring a few young cows back for you," Rock told him.

"That is good. Ames is a good man," James declared.

James introduced the ladies and Rock and Danny greeted them shyly.

The chickens were taken to the barn yard and turned loose, and some grain tossed on the ground. They unhitched the horses and hung the harnesses in the barn this time instead of hanging them on the wagon as they had for many weeks. With every one helping, they took time to curry and brush the horses after watering them. With the other horses and cattle, they turned them all into a small pasture near the corrals. Rock and Danny putting hay out for the animals. There was water in the pasture.

First one horse, then another rolled over and back, groaning like it felt so good. Then they walked around taking a bite of grass then on to another place for a bite.

"Are they tasting to se if it tasted different in different places," Rosalea laughed.

Rosalea and Dawn stood leaning on the fence, watching the animals as they moved around the pasture. James came and stood near.

"Well, welcome home, you beautiful horses," James called to them.

"It looks like they can't believe where they are," Rosalea said. "Like they are looking it over, checking it out."

Dawn; "It must seem different to them, being loose, but in a pasture after all this time."

"King, you are Home, you and all the rest of you wonderful horses," Dawn called to them. King lifted his head and nickered but dropped his head to continue eating.

"We, Danny and I, got us an elk yesterday and we can have some steaks cooked n a few minutes. A pot of beans have been on back of the stove all day. Shouldn't be long 'till we can have supper," Rock called. "I will take some steaks over to our friends," and he did in just a few minutes.

"That will be good. Dawn and I will milk the cows and be in soon," Rosalea said. James went to put out some hay for the horses.

Sitting at the table, James said, "Let us start the first meal with a prayer." He reached his hand to the next one to him, "We hold hands when we pray."

"Our Heavenly Father, we are in our new home here. I pray that you will watch over us all and bless us and bless the ranch and the animals. Thank you for our food and bless it to nourish us. We ask it in Jesus name. Amen."

"Amen," around the table.

James smiled at each one. "Well, now we are really home, thank the Lord. Let's eat this good food, thank you Rock."

"This is elk meat?" Rosalea asked. "It is really good!"

"Yup, it is elk, a young bull," Rock answered. "Got him early yesterday Mornin."

"Oh my, but don't you eat beef?" Dawn asked.

"Yup, shore do. We butcher a steer sometimes. But we get an elk now and then. Just wish you had brought a couple a hogs. Haven't seen Bacon in a long time."

"Why didn't you think of hogs? James," Rosalea asked. "Maybe we could have brought some."

"We did think of it, but couldn't figure out how we could haul them. Our wagons were pretty well loaded and we couldn't have lead them like the cows," he chuckled. "It would have had to be a wagon just for the hogs, and what a mess! Maybe a specially built wagon."

"That's true," Rosalea agreed, thinking of the mess that the hogs would have made.

They lingered, enjoying the food and each other, talking over plans for getting settled.

"Dawn and I will wash the dishes," Rosalea said.

"No 'em, ye won't. Danny and I have it down pat. 'besides, it's getting dark an' you need to fix your beds."

"We will sleep in our beds in the wagon, at leased to night. We are used to that after all of the weeks. And I am tired enough to go right to bed."

But when they went out side, the moon was just up, and it was almost a full moon.

"Oh! Oh look at that moon!' Dawn breathed. "look what it does, shining on the mountains!"

"Dawn, it is so beautiful here! The mountains, the prairie! All this space! Hundreds of miles! We can almost see forever! Hundreds of miles!" Rosalea repeated.

"Look," she exclaimed, pointing out over the prairie, "it looks like it is turned to silver with the moon shining on the grass!"

"And it is our home!" Dawn exclaimed, breathlessly. They sat drinking in the beauty of the night. But the tiredness soon took them to bed.

But in the night, tears came in both of their eyes, remembering the lost husband and father who had so wanted the new home and life in the far west.

Each prayed unspoken prayers for God to help them to make this a good home for them all.

CHAPTER 11

D aylight came, and the rooster was on the top rail of the corral, crowing, flapping his wings and crowing again and again. The hens were busy, singing, clucking and scratching around near by.

Dawn groaned and stretched, "Oh my, I forgot that that rooster could crow!"

"Yes, we will have get used to that, won't we. He must know that this is home. At least he is claiming it," Rosalea laughed. "Come on, let's get up. I think that I heard Rock call breakfast."

"Well, I am as hungry as a bear. I'm up, almost." Dawn said.

Rock stood in the door, "Got to fix a house fur them chickens, some day soon," he laughed. "It is good to have chickens and a rooster 'bout here!" His grin covered his face.

"Breakfast 'bout ready," he called.

"Wash up is on the bench, warm water in the bucket, clean towel hanging there." Rock showed them.

James greeted, "Good morning ladies, sleep good here in our new home?"

"Oh, yes, but it was so quiet, the breeze didn't even whisper!" Dawn exclaimed.

"Well, that can change without warning out here. The wind can really blow sometimes, but there lots of days like this," James said.

"It is so peaceful here," Rosalea said.

"We will hope and pray that it will stay peaceful. There is a kind of strength here. A feeling of being at home, of safety. Like the wind blows away troubles, leaving a cleanness, a deep seated calmness of peace. Something that will last," James agreed.

Breakfast was venison and biscuits and gravy, eaten with relish by the travelers, who were no longer travelers.

Yes, there was a peacefulness yet an eagerness, a stirring to get at things.

They sat with coffee. "James, what do you think that we should do first? Is there time to plant corn and a garden yet? Shall we try?" Rosalea asked.

"Yes, I think that gardens will grow. It is still a few days yet of August. With September and October should stay warm and things should grow. We can try Potatoes and some corn, but maybe not grain. We had better save the seed for next year. I will unload the plow and disk and start. I should have the ground ready to plant in a couple of days. May have trouble with grass coming back but we will try a few potatoes, beans and corn."

James soon had a team hitched to the plow and working on the to be garden spot.

Rosalea and Dawn un-tucked the canvas of the wagon with the potatoes.

"Where is a good place to store the potatoes?" she called to Rock.

"Spuds! Rock exclaimed. "We been out of spuds for a couple of months now."

"I dug a cellar for spuds!" He took them bag after bag and carried them down into a cellar near the back of the house.

"Leave a bag out to use and I am going to cut some to plant," Rosalea told him.

"Sure will be good to have spuds again," Rock declared grinning.

"We will plant a few potatoes and hope they grow yet this summer. We will plant a little corn, hoping that it will grow too, as soon as James gets the ground ready," Rosalea said. "We will want to grow our own."

They continued to unload the food and storing it away, with Rock and Andy's help.

When the barrel of bacon was discovered, Rock let out a shout, "Whooopee, bacon, as I live and breathe, it is real bacon. Now that's for real eating!"

"Wow," Andy murmured from time to time, admiring the different things, as he helped.

"Carrots and beets! And onions! Even cabbages! Can we eat some of these?"

"Yes, indeed we can! We brought seeds to plant to grow for some more for next year," Rosalea told him. "but we are going to eat these!"

"Really?"

"Yup, really!" Dawn answered, ruffling his hair. She thought, 'I'm going to love this young man'. She felt like hugging him, but thought that he might not like that.

Rosalea brought in the bread starter and mixed it up for a big batch of bread to rise for supper.

"That sure smells good!" Rock said. "Recon I can bake bread now!" he grinned at her."

"You want to bake the bread too," Rosalea asked.

"Sure do. I can bake good bread, just didn't have the starter. I lost the starter this spring when a sudden cold spell with snow caught Andy and I out with baby caves that we couldn't leave. We finally got them in to the barn but the fire had gone out and the house as cold as a barn."

They had finished unloading the food and were looking around.

"Mam, the big bedroom is on this side," Rock opened a door. There was a big bed, the frame made from slender logs with branches crisscrossing making a head/board and crossing the bottom to support a mattress, all of the poles and branches pealed and polished shinny.

"Oh my! It is beautiful," Roaslea exclaimed. A small table made from more small logs for legs with a top of a split and smoothed piece from a log. The top of the table was fairly flat, but not really smooth, but Rosalea thought a cloth on top would be good. "It is a good place for a kerosene lamp to sit."

"Who did all of this?" Rosalea asked.

"James. We helped some. We had lot of time in the winter to do things. James wanted things good when you came home."

"Another bedroom off here." Rock walked to the other side of the big main room. He opened the door and stepped back. There stood two beds, smaller, one on each side of the room. The beds were made like the other.

"Who is this room for," Dawn asked.

"Well, for you. He said it was for Dawn. Recon that is you, miss."

"OH my! But why two? There is only me."

"He reckoned that you'd maybe have company sometime. Ames ranch has girls and maybe some will come over sometimes."

"I hope so. I would like to have a friend out here. But how far away is the Ames ranch?" Dawn smiled and asked.

"Bout 20 miles or so."

"Well, we will need to get settled a bit before we go calling on the neighbors, but I am looking forward to doing that."

"Yes, me too," Rosalea agreed.

"Well, they may come soon as they know that you are here. They're good people."

"Well. Dawn, shall we move our beds into the house?" Rosalea asked.

"But Rock and Danny could use this room," Dawn said.

"No'em, Danny and I bunk in the barn for a while. James said that we are going to build a bunk/house before winter. A good bunk/house with a stove and ever thing," Rock declared. "Got to have a bunk/house 'n a few years any way. Going to have some riders when we get more cattle. James said, we are going to have a couple of riders, maybe yet this fall. So might as well get the bunk/house built."

"Now, let's get your beds moved in here."

And with Danny and Rocks help, they were soon moved into the bed/rooms. Rosalea and Dawn each found small forked branches that made hooks, smoothed and attached to the walls making places to hang clothes!

When she commented on them, Rock said; "When I saw some of the ends cut off a branches when we made the beds, they just looked like hooks and we hung them up."

"So you helped to fix all of this!" Dawn exclaimed.

"Well, just a bit. Just helped James some. He's a working man. Don't stop for much. And the winter was long. Had to do some thing."

They had already looked over the living room. The logs were pealed and smooth, well chinked with clay that had dried hard and windproof. The roof of split pieces shaped like shingles but larger. The upper edge of the shingles was mounted with a strip of oiled rawhide under the top edge, making the seam sealed. The roof was supported by pealed logs, and shiny, when looking up at them. There were smaller poles crossing that the hand made shingles were fastened to. There were shingles on the wagon, waiting. Maybe they wouldn't be needed on the house for a few years. But the bunk/house when it was built could use them.

CHAPTER 12

James and John had been blessed with a keg of nails that Joe Ames had left and they had made good use of them in building.

The table was about 8 feet long with the top of slabs of logs and smoothed as well as could be done without a wood plane to smooth them. Rosalea remembered that she had seen a couple of wood planes somewhere in the load. Then she remembered that there were planks, nice and smooth, on the wagon and Tom had said that they would make a nice table. But, oh she liked this one! It was quite smooth and a cloth could cover it. There were shelves on one wall, maybe for books. Yes they had brought a few books, but only a few. More shelves in the kitchen area held a few tin plates and a couple of kettles. A big cook stove that Joe Ames had given them, and a smaller table close, took up a large place on that wall A skillet hung behind the stove. Two bunks along one wall. They were not very wide and Rosalea and Dawn decided that with pillows against the wall, they could be couches for sitting as well for added napping or be a place for sleeping. They would be good that way for winter/ time. If the bunkhouse didn't get built, Rock and Danny could sleep on those two couches, quite comfortably. They had slept there before.

There were window openings but they were covered with some hides. The new windows were on a wagon, waiting to be installed! A door at the back of the house opened into a long lean/to that was nearly full of firewood.

"Rock, will you help me to get a barrel out of the wagon," Rosalea asked.

It was soon in the house and Rosalea was unpacking dishes and washing the tin cups and plates them to put on the shelves in the kitchen. The rest of the barrel with the good dishes would have to wait for more shelves and to use later. She had Rock move it back against the wall, out of the way. With the lid back on the barrel could be used to set the dutch oven on.

"How about fried bacon and spuds for dinner? I would sure like that," Rock said. "I am still going to be cook around here if you will let me."

"If you want to cook, I will let you," Rosalea laughed. James had warned her that Rock took his job as cook seriously. There would be times when the chuck wagon would be needed out on the range, cooking was his contribution to the work around the ranch. He with one leg a bit stiff, he had difficulty riding a horse. But Rock helped around the barns and corrals, anywhere something needed to be done. James had said that Rock was a hard worker and that Danny, although he was young, he was willing and given a job he would do a good job.

Dawn was drying the dishes and setting the table.

"I smell bacon!" James was walking in the door.

Dinner was soon on the table and enjoyed by all.

"I think that I have a big enough spot plowed to plant for now. I will disk it a couple times this afternoon, and disk it again a couple of times tomorrow too. Hopefully that will soon make it good for planting."

"A table cloth from home! Looks good, like home is gong to be good out here in our new home. I see pots and pans too. You like that, Rock?"

"You bet! It is good to have more than a couple of pans," he laughed. "And look at the size of this skillet! Big enough for a mess of spuds!"

James bowed his head, "Father God, we thank you for this time of us being together in our new home, and thank you for this good food. Bless it and bless our home." He stopped, unable to go on, thinking of the missing one. A shaky "Amen."

"Amen" was heard around the table.

They followed James when he went back to the garden with the disk.

"James, this looks like a really good garden place," Rosalea exclaimed.

"Yes, I thought so. Josh and Jereme are going to help and we will all help work and have a garden big enough for us all here."

"That is a good idea," Rosalea said. They all went to the garden again as soon as dishes were done and everything cleaned up. Rock and Danny refused to let the girls wash dishes.

Fresh bread was the highlight for supper, with more venison and mashed potatoes and gravy with boiled beets. Andy smiled and sighed all through dinner.

"Boy, we are living high on the hog now!" Rock exclaimed happily. Everyone laughed with him.

The next morning after the milking was done and strained and into covered cans, Rosalea said, "All of this milk! It will go to waste! I am going to take some to town for them." Which she did, sharing it with each house. She was greeted warmly and thanked for the milk.

"You brought so much!" Molly told her.

"Maybe you can make cottage cheese with some."

"I will! I surely will! It has been a while since we have had milk."

"I will bring some milk every other day," Rosalea told her.

John arrived with his parents the next day and they were exclaiming with wonder over their new home and glad to be at the end of the long trip.

The next time to bring the milk was Sunday and they all loaded into the wagon and went to town and to attend church. John brought all of the Obeys too.

They were greeted and welcomed. But instead of standing in the pulpit, Jonathon Brooks gathered them near and sat with them. "Let's talk about Our Lord, Maybe share some of the things He has done for us." They did and the time passed swiftly and Molly Craft finally said, "I have a kettle of stew on the back of the stove, and fresh bread, come, let us go eat."

The after noon was spent talking and getting acquainted sitting in Molly's big room.

"We have cows to milk, so we must go before dark," Rosalea said.

"I have been thinking, how about us bringing one of the cows and you keep her here and you milk her and have the milk here fresh every day."

"That would be wonderful, if you are sure?" Molly said. "I have a barn out back and a big pasture that I haven't had any use for. Will is going to try to get some milk cows and hogs. While the men didn't have much to do they fixed a place to be ready for the animals. And we have grain we can feed her. The milk will be good when the wagon trains start coming too!"

"You can skim off the cream and make butter and use the skim milk for the cottage cheese too if there is enough milk." Roaslea said.

"We have too much milk too," Lilly said. We can bring one of our cows too. We just have to dump milk and I hate to do that. When we were with the wagon train, we shared with others and it didn't go to waste."

"Maybe I can make some butter every day or two and put it in the cellar. The cellar is really cool and it should keep for weeks." Molly said. "Then when the wagon trains come, we will have butter for them."

"Those on the wagon trains will be overjoyed to get milk and butter after all the time of the trail," Will Culbert said. "I think we have a good thing here. Thank to you. We will surely give you credit."

"I wasn't thinking of any credit," Rosalea said, "I just hate to have the milk go to waste. And if it will help you, that will be good. We can help each other. We will still have plenty of milk and cream and butter for our own use. And we give some of the cottage cheese to the chickens."

"Me too," Lilly said

"I will take care of the cows and milk them, my contribution to the project." Jonathan injected.

"I will help where ever I can, and be glad to have something to do," Saraha Brooks said.

"I may need your help when the wagon trains come," Molly told her.

"Oh! I will be glad to help," Saraha agreed.

"I think that we will bake bread and as long as we have sugar, maybe a few cakes," Molly added.

We have lots of flour, and there will be more flour and sugar when the freight comes," Will said.

Will had been grinning, then, "You know, we won't really need to charge them much for the milk and butter. We will be getting so much good for ourselves."

"Charge just enough that they think that they are paying, because most people want to pay for what they get," John said.

"And there may be some who can't pay much. It could help them to go on west.

"That is true. Maybe just a little for the milk and butter can help pay for the hogs when they come, and any leftover milk can be fed to the hogs when they get here," James said.

"Another community project? We can raise hogs and butcher and cure bacon to sell too. And have bacon for our selves."

"Ha ha, what a good idea James! And see what friends and neighbors can do working together!" Will clapped his hands.

"And think how the travelers will be blessed by getting fresh milk after such a long time, and especially the butter." Molly said.

"We are going to have a wonderful place here with you people coming," Molly added, looking at each one. "It was lonesome with just the 5 of us."

"Amen to that," Jonathan declared enthusiastically.

"Well, we are blessed and will continue be more so when we need some things and you order them and have them shipped. We hadn't dreamed that could be possible for maybe years," James said.

The next day found James with Josh and Jereme helping to take the two cows to Molly's pasture.

CHAPTER 13

They had planted potatoes and some corn and a couple of hills of squash and beans. Every day Rosalea and Dawn were checking for weeds and grass around the new plants that came up and were growing fast. They were ruthless on weeds and the grass that crept between the plants.

With all of the needed work, the days flew by.

John and James were busy putting in the windows and the new doors into the houses. Then John and his father were busy building another room for his parents. John was glad for the lumber and building materials that they had brought. It was making the home comfortable as well as beautiful. He had installed the big cook stove as soon as he got home. Josh and Jereme helping wherever they could, often riding out to check on the cattle and horses. They spent a lot of time in the saddle.

James and Rock were cutting and hauling logs for the bunkhouse. Danny helping where ever he could, making his rounds where something was happening.

Rock continued to do all of the cooking and baking the bread. There were never any complaints, he was a good cook, and the meals were enjoyed by all.

Lilly, Rosalea and Dawn spent time, busy washing clothes and blankets, things that needed to be clean after the long trip when sometimes everything wasn't washed. They wanted everything clean before it was stored for the rest of the summer and to be ready for the coming winter. This took days, getting things clean and dry.

They dug out dresses and hung them up, ready to wear around the house while the weather was warm. But summer was waning, the fall would soon be here. They still were wearing the boy's clothes, out petting and grooming the horses and riding out to get acquainted with the surrounding area.

Days went by with short rides looking at the rolling prairie. One day, James and Danny would ride with them and they went to ask Lilly and the boys if they wanted to go riding. John and his father were still building on the house. Rock declined to go, "My stiff leg isn't so good for riding. I am going to check on the garden, can't let weeds get ahead of us."

Lilly and the boys went with them, so there was a group riding out. First they went to check on the cattle and found them feeding near the small stream within a mile of the buildings. The other horses were near by. King raised his head and nickered at Dawn's call, and stood watching her. She waved at him and said, "It is O.K. King, we don't need you now."

"We will need to ride King now and then too," James said.

They were remembering that King had been Tom's horse.

As if King understood he continued to graze.

"The cattle are looking good," James said. "The calves are getting pretty well grown."

"Oh look at the calves," Dawn exclaimed. They were running and jumping around, chasing each other, which brought a laugh from them all.

"These are heifer calves," James explained.

"Oh. They are so sleek and pretty!"

James showed and told them about the different areas. They talked about the abundance of the tall grass covering the prairie.

"James, we could have hundreds of cattle here, with all of this grass!" Rosalea exclaimed.

"Yes, That is my dream," James agreed.

"We have money to buy more!" Rosalea said. When can we do that?"

"We can buy them in the Fall when we take the steers to sell. Hopefully there will be some young cows to buy." James answered. "Sometimes in the spring or summer, Joe Ames takes a bunch of older cows and bulls to sell and brings home some young stock. Maybe next year I could go along with them and buy what we want and bring back."

"We can buy some more cattle too?" Lilly asked.

"Yes, John plans to buy cattle too. But you know, our cows will be having calves and our herd will increase without buying any more. Maybe in another year we won't need to buy any more cows. Our herd will increase it's self more each year. And we will have steers to sell each fall. Maybe we will wait and sell every other year. A two year old will bring a lot more money. It may sound like 'counting our chickens before they hatch,' but looking ahead at the possibilities, it looks good."

"Oh, yes! I can see your dreams for the future here," Rosalea said.

"Gosh!" Josh exclaimed in wonder. But that was all he could say. He sat looking at the cattle and then his eyes scanned the surrounding prairie, mentally envisioning many cattle out on the grass.

They followed the river for several miles towards the mountains and discovered a lake, and above the lake a few miles, found where the river swept between steep cliffs. They could see grass land on the other side then breaks with canyons off a ways in the distance.

"Who owns that land on the other side of the river?" Dawn asked.

"It is open land, no one owns it."

"So much land!" Roasalea exclaimed. "Miles and miles of grass land!"

"Yes, that is what John and I discovered and decided that we want to live here," James said, enthusiasm in his voice.

They stopped at the lake on the return trip and it was as cold as ice.

"Well, that's for that. No swimming in this lake," Dawn said, disappointedly. "I was sure hoping to have a place to swim."

They had been gone for hours and were ravishingly hungry when they got home just in time to hurry with chores before supper.

Rock, standing in the door, called to them, "supper is ready. There is enough for all, come join us Lilly and boys."

"Thanks Rock, but I had better go see if Mom needs help," Lilly answered.

CHAPTER 14

A few days later Lilly told Rosalea, "I have made butter and we put some in the cellar and still have much, do you suppose that a wagon train has come by yet and maybe they could use some more at the store?"

"Me too. I will take it over and see. Anyway, Molly's cellar is really cold and it will keep till they need it. Do you want to go along?"

"No, it is pretty busy at our house with the building. Maybe next time."

Rosalea and Dawn took the butter and a can of the morning's fresh milk and Lilly's extra.

They were warmly welcomed. Molly said, "A wagon train left this morning and they said that another train is coming a few days behind them. So the butter will sure be welcome. I am completely out of milk and butter. The people were overjoyed at getting the milk and butter and there was so many of them, they took everything that I had. I gave them all of the cottage cheese too."

"We will bring more in a couple of days," Rosalea assured her. "First one then another cow goes dry in the winter before they have another calf. So we will all have less milk in the winter time."

The next day Will Culbert came out with bad news. He wanted to talk to both James and John.

He told them, "A rider came and said that the Ames outfit were bringing cattle home and were attacked and some of them hurt and a couple killed and the cattle stolen and scattered. Ames sent word to ask if you could come help gather cattle. The rider was going on to the TXT ranch for help too."

"We will head out immediately," James told him.

James called Rock and Danny, "Rock, outfit the chuck wagon and follow us as soon as you can. Put your rifle handy and take guns and ammunition and be prepared. Danny, saddle your horse but stay with Rock. Put a scabbard and rifle on the saddle and a couple bags of oats and help put a water barrel on the wagon. Be prepared to defend yourselves. Hurry as fast as you can. Hopefully we will meet you and be coming back with the cattle, but it may take time to gather the cattle so look for us."

John, James and Josh and Jereme were soon gone.

The women helped to get the chuck wagon ready. Rock tossed in bedrolls for all. Rock and Danny were soon following.

The three women and John's older parents were home alone.

"We will remember to pray," Rosalea said as they left Lilly.

"The milk is already in the wagon. Let's take it to the store."

They had delivered the milk and were talking in the store when 6 men rode in at a gallop, sliding to a halt, scattering dust. They were ragged, scruffy looking, covered with dust.

"Got any tabacca in this here store?" one asked as he swaggered into the store. The rest of the men followed, one at a time, looking around as they entered. They could see that there were three men in the store and looked them over. Dan was standing behind the counter near Will. Jonathan was seated near the women.

"Yup, shore do," Will said, "Smoking or chawin?"

"Smokin" three of the men said. "Chawin," the others said.

"Well, we've got both," Will said, reaching up on a shelf for it.

"Any thing else?" Will asked.

"No. Not this time."

The men each dropped the coins on the counter, picking up their tobacco.

The men left, slowly, one at a time, looking around as they went.

Will and Dan followed them to the door and watched them ride away.

"I don't much like the looks of that bunch," Dan said.

"Nor do I," Will said. "I believe that we need to be on the watch. They might come back."

"Keep a gun handy, Will." Dan cautioned.

"Yes, each one of us." Will went into a back room and returned with a pistol, with a holster and some shells. He handed it to Jonathan, "Know how to use this?"

"Yes," Jonathan said slowly.

"Put it on and wear it most of the time. And keep it handy at night."

"You think that there may be a need for this?"

"I have a hunch that there could be, by the way that those men looked around and at each of us." He went back and returned with more guns and holsters and boxes of shells.

"One for each of the rest of you," he started handing them to each of the women.

"Do you know how to handle these?" he asked.

"Yes, but do we women need to?" Lilly asked.

"Maybe you more than us men. Put these on and wear them most of the time," repeating the cautioning to Jonathan.

"We have rifles at home," Rosalea.

"Well, keep them handy as well," Will said.

A few days later, Rosalea and Dawn were again delivering milk and butter to the store. They stood talking when another bunch of men rode in.

Rosalea remembered that She and Dawn had forgotten and left the guns at home.

The men rode in like they owned the place, their horses rearing and stomping, snorting, shaking their heads trying to ease the tightly held bits in their mouths.

The men were laughing and shouting. As the dust began to settle, they looked around and seen the women.

"Well fellers, look what we have here! A couple a good looking ladies," the leader of the group said.

"I get first pick," another one said.

"And where are your husbands, Ladies," the first one said. "Or do you have any. Some don't last long in this country," his laugh was harsh and guttural.

"Our husbands are coming in soon," Rosalea said. "We are meeting them here."

"Well, now, we saw some men out a ways and they was busy chasing cattle," he laughed. "I don't think they will be in soon." He threw his head back and laughed loudly. He threw his leg over and jumped from his horse and started towards Rosalea.

"I'm picking this one," the second man jumped off of his horse and started towards Dawn.

They hadn't heard them, but 2 men had quietly ridden in and stepping down from their horses and came to the girls. The older of the young men walked over to Rosalea and put his arm around her.

"This lady is MY wife," he said quietly. Rosalea, startled, looked up at him, she was trembling and he tightened his arm, pulling her against his side. He looked down into brown eyes with golden glints. A wealth of dark red/brown hair, lit up with gold, surrounded her face and extended down her back nearly to her waist.

Rosalea looked into the deep blue of the sky of his eyes.

"And THIS pretty girl is MY wife." The younger man walked over to Dawn putting his arm around her. Dawn gasped and he held her tighter and kissing her hair whispered in her ear, "easy, it's O.K."

He looked down and into such brown eyes! eyes that gold lights gleamed in them as Dawn looked up into the startling deep blue of the sky of his eyes.

Looking back at the leader of the bunch; "You fellers go around bothering and insulting ladies, you may not last long in this country." The older man said.

The men's arms were still around the girls, holding them against their left side. Their right hand near the holstered gun.

A group of men quietly rode in behind the outfit and stopped. An older man with white hair sparkling in the black, spoke, "What is going on here, Pete?" His voice was almost deadly quiet.

"Just a bunch of drifters and about to drift along. They were insulting our wives. I think that maybe they are about to apologize and head out again."

The older man said, "If I remember right these ladies would probably teach these fellers some manners. Turn 'em loose boys. Here Daughter, catch this gun, it's fully loaded." He tossed a six-gun to Rosalea, and she was amazed that she caught it. She righted it in her hand, pointing it at the ground in front of the leader's horse. She moved her left hand over to the pistol as though as pull the hammer back.

The men jumped aboard and kicking their horses and again scattering dust as they galloped away.

The grinning men dismounted.

"Mam, do you know my sons?" coming to Rosalea.

"No, but I am sure glad they came when they did," she said as she handed the gun back.

"I think that you ladies should carry guns and learn to shoot. We have seen a couple of bunches of questionable characters around these parts lately. Seen them at a distance as though they wouldn't pass inspection of a closer look. I am Tony Ogerly from the TXT ranch, out west about 50 miles. My son Pete and my son Paul," he indicated the two.

"We will wear the guns from now on," Rosalea assured him.

Pete spoke; "Forgive me for getting so personal, Mam. I thought it might be best. Two guns against 6 is not so good, with you two ladies in danger."

"Pete Ogerly, thank you for what you did." She reached for his hand, grasping it and clinging to it for a long moment. "There is nothing to forgive. It was very thoughtful of you to help us. I was really scared." Rosalea said.

She turned back to the older man; "Mr. Ogerly thank you all. I am Rosalea Larson and my Daughter Dawn. We have a ranch out a ways. And have you met these people here at the store?"

"Yes, but we haven't been in for a while. How are you all doing?" he reached to shake Will Culbert's hand. The others had stayed back but came to greet him.

"We," Ogerly indicated his riders. "came to warn you about that outfit. We had seen them at a distance. They left when they seen us. Then they came here. And there's another bunch of no good men around too." After greeting the others he turned back to Rosalea; "Where are your husbands?"

"My husband was killed weeks ago on the way here. Dawn is not married. My brother James Larson had word of trouble for the Ames outfit who are bringing some cattle home to their ranch and James went to find them and help. Mr. Culbert can explain."

After Culbert's report, Tony Ogerly stood a moment, frowning.

"The Ames outfit? They have a pretty good crew of riders. Must have been a big bunch that attacked them, probably from ambush."

"Boys;" he turned to his riders, "Tim, you stay here with Culberts' outfit. Pete and Paul, take these ladies home and be sure every thing is alright at the ranch. The rest of us are going out to find the Ames and Larsons. Keep your eyes open, men. Those fellers that were just here could have been involved and may come back."

They galloped away, following the wagon trail that lead back towards the east. At a good distance they found where the cattle and chuck wagon had turned off to north/west.

"They turned off here towards the Ames ranch," Ogerly stated.

Putting their horses at a mile eating easy lope, they followed the trail for some time, coming upon where an attack had occurred. The chuck wagon stood, the horses dead, still hooked to the wagon, the driver dead, another horse and rider dead.

"It must have been a quick attack, and the cattle run off. Some of the Ames riders are following. And look here more wagon tracks and a couple more horses following." Ogerly stated.

"Some one else has followed them," one of his men said.

Ogerly said. "Larson's outfit."

They galloped away following the tracks and soon seen a chuck wagon ahead, traveling at a rapid trot.

"Whoa," Ogerly called. "Hey! We are from the TXT. Stop."

Rock pulled the team to a stop. "Glad to see you fellers. Things look pretty rough for our crew," he called.

"Indeed it does," Ogerly agreed. "You had better not get involved, you and the boy."

"Some one needs to help," Rock protested.

"That is what my men and I are going to do. You turn off here and head straight north. You should hit the Ames ranch. You can report what you know and go on home to watch out for the women at your ranch. The trail is going to be too rough real soon for the wagon to go much farther."

"Thank God that you are on their trail. Be careful yourselves," Rock told them. But Rock sat thinking as the men rode off.

"I don't think that we will do that, Danny. I think that we will go on and follow James and John. Maybe we can help."

They followed the trail and seen where the TXT had turned off, leaving the trail of the cattle that they were sure that John and James and the boys were following. The trail continued for a few miles and dropped down into a narrow entrance to a canyon too steep for the wagon. They suddenly could hear shots. Rock set the break on the wagon, jumped off. He tied the team to a bush and grabbed the rifle and started for the canyon.

"Come with me, Danny, but stay behind me," Rock started on with a half running limp, swinging his nearly stiff leg. Danny was on his horse and kept pace just behind Rock, his rifle in his hand.

More shots and a horse came running out of the canyon and straight up to them. Danny spurred his horse and caught the bridle and stopped the horse.

"This is James' horse," Rock exclaimed. She was skittish and shook her head and moved restlessly, obviously nervous. Rock spoke to her and patted her. She began to calm. He shoved his rifle in the scabbard and slowly climbed into the saddle.

Another horse came running and Rock reached and grabbed the bridle and leading it, started for the canyon.

"Oh God, the shooting has stopped! Come on Danny!" Rock kicked the horse into a run towards the opening of the canyon.

He drew her up and slowed to a stop as they came within sight of the valley.

Men were shouting, "Hello Ames, TXT here."

Rock could see Joe Ames and heard him call, "Hello TXT, Ames here! You sure a welcome sight."

Rock, going on, could see James sitting on the ground, with his rifle still in his hands.

Rock slid off the horse, "James, are your hurt?"

"Not much, I think."

They were soon surrounded by men checking on the two wounded men. They discovered that James' leg had been broken. His horse had thrown him. Rocks had hit her in the face from a bullet hitting the rocks right in front of her. She had reared and James had been thrown against some rocks. James had a slicing wound in his left arm from bullet clipping the arm.

CHAPTER 15

Back to the TXT; as they continued to follow the trail of the cattle.

"Boss, remember a few years ago that canyon where we found those cattle thieves with our cattle?"

Ogerly drew his horse to a halt. "I will never forget that," he answered.

"Boss, maybe this outfit is headed there to that canyon."

"That is likely. It must be the same canyon."

"We went in the other way and caught them as they came into the canyon."

"O.K., boys, let's try that again. We know that it is not the same bunch. They are still in there, under some rocks."

They raced around and as they were entering the hidden canyon, they could hear shots. Rounding some rocks there were cattle scattered, wild eyed, milling frantically around. They could see that some men were shooting at others that had just entered the canyon on the other side.

"These have to be the outlaws here in the rocks. They have the Ames outfit pinned down." Ogerly shouted "Get 'em boys" as he opened fire, picking out the men that were hiding from the Ames' but were not hidden from them. It was soon over.

"Hello, Ames, the TXT here," Ogerly shouted.

"Hello TXT, Ames here. You are sure a welcome sight!"

They discovered that one of the Ames riders and James Larson were injured. After examined, neither seriously hurt. After binding up flesh wounds, they found that James had a broken leg.

Rock was there and said that he had a chuck wagon near by and he could haul the wounded men. Ames insisted that they were to take them to the closest place for care, which was the Ames ranch.

"We will bring the cattle home at a more leisurely pace," Ogerly told them.

When Rock with James and the wounded rider arrived at the Ames ranch, Mrs. Ames and her oldest daughter, Connie, took over and the men were promptly put into bed and the wounds retreated.

James was glad that he didn't need to ride any farther. He was quite weak and thanking Connie, he closed his eyes and promptly fell asleep.

His stay at the Ames ranch would continue for several weeks. James, while he mended, was getting acquainted with the incredible blue eyes that he remembered from the years in the past. Eyes such a deep blue they were almost purple.

Mean while, Back at the Culbert store:

"Tim, you and Will and Dan, keep an eye out and have everyone to be ready to go into one building and everyone spend the nights there where it will be easier to watch and guard," Pete suggested.

"We can use my place," Molly said.

"We have rifles and guns and can watch," Culbert said. "We will watch and be alright."

Pete and Paul looked their approval as they rode into the Larson/Obey ranch. "This is going to be a good spread. How many hands do you have?"

"There is James and John Obey and their two sons. And John's dad and Mom are here. His parents are older. We have an older man, Rock, who took the chuck wagon and Danny, a young lad about 10 years old went with him to try to catch up with James and the rest," Rosalea answered.

"Now, it is just you two girls, Mrs. Obey and the old parents at home here?"

"Yes, until James, John and the rest get home."

"Mr. Ogerly," Rosalea said softly, "There is a rider off over on that rise over past the corral."

"Yes, I see him. There were 4 of them. You girls go on into the house and stay put. I don't know how many there are but it's probably that bunch that was at the store. Paul will go bring the Obeys over here. Let's try to make it look like they are just coming over for supper but then they should stay the night here. Paul and I will watch and see how many of them there are and what they are doing."

"That nice young man said that you want us to come for supper, Rosalea," the older lady said, as they entered the house.

"Yes, we thought that we would like some company for a while. Sit down. I will make some coffee and we will have supper soon."

Pete and Paul unhitched the team and put the horses in the corral. There own horses they put into stalls but left them saddled, loosening the cinches a bit and taking the bits out, leaving the bridles on but the horses could eat. The horses could be ready to ride at any moment. The men started working around the barn and corrals, putting down hay, feeding chickens. Doing things like it was general work, all the while watching men who were watching them.

Pete speaking softly said, "I see 6 men, maybe the outfit we saw in town."

"Yes, that is what I see. But why are they here, if they think that we are the women's husbands? That this is our ranch. Do they think that they can attack and get away with?" Paul asked.

"I think that maybe they think that they can sneak in and steal horses during the night. Their horses look pretty badly abused."

"They sure do."

"We will make it look like we are in the house to stay for the night. Later we can come and hide out here and be prepared to defend the place."

"I saw a nest of eggs, I'll get them, then let's go in the house."

"Brought in some eggs," Pete handed Rosalea his hat with the eggs.

She looked her surprise but thanked him.

Pete Ogerly walked over and stood in front of the older Obeys.

"Mr. And Mrs. Obey, Rosalea and Dawn know, but I want to tell you; there were a group of tough looking men at the store. They left the store but there are some men who seem to be hiding, not far off and watching the ranch. I think that they are the same men, and up to no good. Like I said they are staying pretty much hidden but we have seen them from time to time. I don't know what they are doing out there, but they may plan to steal horses. They saw us come into the house. We will wait a while and sneak out to the barn and wait to see if they try to come down. You plan to stay here all night and all of you stay in the house. Can any of you use a gun if you might need to?"

"Yes," from each. "We have guns here in the house," Rosalea told him.

"Hopefully you won't need them, but keep them handy. We will call out when we come back, so don't shoot us." Pete grinned.

"I am going out on the roof and see if I can see them," Paul said. "On this side of the roof, they can't see me if I am careful."

In a few minutes he came back. "Let's go Pete, they have moved away some and started a fire."

Pete told them, "We won't be in for a while, maybe not all night, but don't worry."

"But you didn't get any supper," Rosalea protested.

"Just a couple of chunks of that bread will do for now," Pete grinned. "It smells pretty good."

Rosalea spread butter on some big hunks of the bread for them. They grinned and thanked her.

They slid out of the door, and watching, went to the barn and crawling onto the hay, settling for a stay.

"Boy, this is good bread," Paul grinned.

Later, "Wake me up if I fall to sleep."

Pete woke. They both had fallen asleep. He had turned in his sleep and poked a bit of hay into his cheek. He came fully awake. He reached to Paul and touched him. Paul moved, then jerked awake.

"Easy," Pete whispered. "We both slept. Careful, lets get out of this hay. It's too noisy."

They both eased out of the hay and stood, picking bits of hay off. A nearly full moon had come up and hung in the sky, lighting things up quite clearly. They could see the horses in the corral, munching hay. Other wise quiet prevailed. Looking around, they could see some rolled up ropes hung at the end of the shed. There were two sticks two inches diameter, about arms length long, leaning just inside the shed.

Paul motioned towards the top of the loafing shed. Pete nodded and motioned to come on. Climbing on the corral poles they hoisted them selves to the roof of the shed. One at near each end of the roof, they lay down. Soon they seen movement. Two men were creeping down the hill towards the corral. They slid off the roof and stepped back into the shadow. Pete stepped close to Paul and whispered, "Let's knock them out." Pete handed one of the sticks to Paul and taking the other stick, stepped a short distance away. The two men coming creeping along, were about the same distance apart as Pete and Paul. As soon as they were near enough, they were struck almost at the same time and the men fell without making a sound. They quickly tied their hands and feet and pulled their neck bandanas tight over their mouths, then drug them over and slid them into a cellar.

Back they went into the shadows. They picked up the sticks again. It was some time before more men came.

A whispered; "Where are you fellers?"

"Here," Paul whispered.

"Where, I can't see in the dark."

"Here," both whispered.

The men moved toward the dark to be met with the sticks, and soon joined the other two.

Back to waiting. "Two more to go."

"But maybe they won't come."

"Then we go after them."

Soon, a harsh whisper—"Where the h—are you men?"

Two soft clunks answered.

Paul and Pete retrieved the rest of the men out of the cellar and putting ropes around them under the arms and the rope up their backs, they hung them to the pole at the top of the loafing shed. There they hung, securely bound hand and feet, unconscious, their chins drooping to their chests.

"Now what are we going to do with them?" Paul asked.

"I think that these are the men that that sheriff from Texas is looking for. I think that we will borrow Rosalea's wagon in the morning and take them and find that Texas law man."

They left the men pretty much trussed up like they were and put them in the wagon and hauled them away. The bandanas had come loose and they had to listened to some severe cursing until Paul reached over with one of the sticks that had quieted them before and tapped them a time or two and finally quiet took over. They found the lawman just leaving the Culbert store. He thanked them for capturing the outlaws.

Later the Texas Ranger, with a wagon bought from Culbert, was well on his way returning to Texas with the wanted men, who were trussed and up pretty well secured, unable to move much. The Ranger's saddle horses were tied behind the wagon.

When Pete and Paul returned with the wagon, they found the Obeys and Rosalea and Dawn eating breakfast. The men had not returned.

"You all watch and wait for some of us to return. We are going to go find the others." Pete told them.

Rosalea insisted that Paul and Pete sit down and eat first.

Retrieving their horses Pete and Paul headed out to find out why no one had returned. At the store, Culbert had not seen any of the men returning from the attack on the Ames outfit.

Pete and Paul in heading out, followed the trail for some time, then came to where they found the trail of the cattle and it turned to the north/west.

"They are headed for the Ames ranch, Paul said.

They found where the attack had occurred. The chuck wagon stood there, the horses dead, still hitched to the wagon. The dead driver, hanging over the front of the wagon. There was a dead horse, the saddle and bridle still on the horse, the dead rider near by.

"There has been quite a fight here. I wonder if Dad and the boys were in on it."

"No, I don't think so. I think the battle would have been over here if the TXT outfit were in on it."

"This is the Ames chuck wagon," Paul said. "But look here is another set of wagon tracks, going on following the cattle tracks. And it looks like more horse tracks, joining the trail."

They followed the signs off to the west following the tail of cattle and horses.

"It looks like they were running here," Paul said.

"And a chuck wagon is following. But why west? The outlaws must still be chasing the cattle here."

"They are headed into canyon country to hide the cattle."

They followed the tracks of the driven cattle and found a deserted chuck wagon, horses tethered to a tree. The trail lead on down through rough country and coming into a deep and steep canyon. Then they could hear shooting. They were entering the canyon. Then a shout.

"That is Dad, but where are they?"

"Well it sounds like the battle is over, now. Now that Dad and the men are here." They entered the steep rocky canyon and came upon rancher Ames with their Dad coming from up the canyon towards him.

"You beat us here, Dad, and have taken care of the situation quite well," Pete said. Rock and Danny were there.

"We have the chuck wagon near. We can haul the men in it," Rock told them.

After the wounded men were cared for and carried out to the chuck wagon. Ames again, insisted that they be taken to the Ames ranch near by.

Pete and Paul were going to help bring the cattle out of the canyons and on to the ranch. "Dad, you and the boys go ahead on home, Paul and I can manage to take these few cattle on over to the Larson/Obey ranch."

Riding leisurely, side by side, Pete said, "You know, Paul, I liked it when I said that Rosalea was my wife. I keep thinking about it."

"I know what you mean. Felt pretty good. I liked the feeling of protecting her. Protecting a woman, a good feeling," Paul said.

"Yes, holding her in my arm and protecting her, God! that felt good! And her eyes! Gold and brown eyes!" Pete exclaimed.

"They are beautiful aren't they. The girls are beautiful! Like Mom! She reminds me of Mom, don't you think so?" from Paul.

"That's right! She does remind me of Mom. Mom is still beautiful! Dad is so lucky to have a woman like Mom. Good old Dad! He is a good man." Pete declared.

"For us to have a woman like Mom! Wouldn't that be some thing!"

"Where could we find any other girls way out here. Do you think that they might look at a couple of fellows like us?" Paul said hesitantly.

Pete looked at his brother, "You know, Paul, you are a pretty good looking man."

"You really think so? You are better to look at than I am."

"I think that we could pass. How do we go about it? I don't know what to do. Some how we need to win them. And before some of the other men around find them."

"Well, we will just have to show up around where they are. Some how show them that we are the men that they need."

"I suppose that we have to go home and see what Dad says about it. The ranch is big enough to take care of us all with wives and kids."

"Kids! Oh my God! Kids! I hadn't got so far as to think of kids! Me! Me! To have kids, children! OOOh!"

111

"I know! But that happens when you get married. Look at what Dad and Mom did. There are 8 of us 'kids'!"

"You are the oldest and I am the youngest. You haven't looked for a girl?" Paul asked.

"I haven't had time to even think about girls, women. The Ames have a couple of girls." Pete answered. "But I guess that I never looked very close at them. I think that they are pretty enough. And it is a good family, a good ranch."

They fell quietly into private thoughts, thinking of what they could do to win the lady of their heart.

CHAPTER 16

Mean while back at the ranch, Dawn found her mother working in the garden. She told her mother, "I'm going out to feed animals."

"Alright, I am going to work here for a while yet," Rosalea answered.

Rosalea continued pulling weeds and then took a hoe and began to stir the soil around the plants. "Thank you Lord for these good days for the garden to grow. It will be so good to have the potatoes and the corn. And the beans are a foot high! The corn is nearly 2 feet high! And look at these big fat leaves of the potatoes!"

She stood, enjoying the warm day. She looked up at the blue sky. "It is so beautiful here! The sky is so blue!"

Blue eyes, almost as blue as the sky, came to her memory. "Those blue eyes! Those blue eyes are Peter Ogerly's eyes!" Her mouth flew open! "How can I think like this way of Peter Oglery," she chided her self. "Tom has only been gone for a couple of months."

She remembered Tom's last words to her. He had repeated over and over,

"Promise me that you will make a new life, a new life." She remembered that he had made her promise again, and again that she would make a new life. The memory startled her.

Was something reminding her of the promise? She had never thought of another man to ever be in her life.

She slid to the ground and put her face into the grass, and began to cry.

"Tom, I can't ever have another man in my life. You are my life." How she wept, the tears flooded her eyes and washed her face. Finally, the crying spent, she sat up and her eyes returned to the blue sky, and the blue eyes returned to her inner sight.

She could hear the words; "You promised me to make a new life," in Tom's voice.

"Maybe some day, Tom, but not soon," she told him.

She sat there a while and prayed. What she prayed, she couldn't remember later. But peace flooded her.

At last she took up the hoe and gently smoothed the dirt that she had been chopping up around the plants.

After talking to her mother, Dawn had gone back to the house.

The men had not returned yet, so she strapped on the pistol and taking a rifle, went to the barn. She discovered that the horses were missing from the pasture. The gate, lay open, thrown wide.

"Some one has stolen our horses! Oh I wish that Paul and Pete were here to help us!" She was remembering, Paul with his arm around her, protecting her. "His blue eyes!" she exclaimed. "His eyes as blue as the deep blue sky!" She raised her eyes and looking at the deep blue of the sky, seeing the blue of his eyes. She would never forget those eyes. She had been so scared, yet Paul's arm around her had made her feel safe. Her shoulder against his chest, she remembered the feel of it.

"I sure wish you were here now, Paul," she said, then laughed.

"Well, Paul isn't here now, so it is up to me to be the cowgirl that can go find the horses."

Her mare, Penny, was still standing in the barn where she had left her. Dawn saddled her and shoved the rifle into the scabbard.

"Come on Penny, we are going for a ride." She could see, though they were dim, the tracks leaving the pasture and heading out to the north/west. She stopped to throw a shell into the chamber of the rifle, "O.K. now we are ready, Penny. Let's go find our horses!"

The trail was easy to follow and she could see it quite a ways ahead. She put Penny into an easy lope that would eat up the miles but not tire her too much. She noticed that the trail lead along the way that they had traveled when they had ridden out looking over the land. Then, the trail turned, going toward the river. She followed and found where they had crossed the river. Evidently they had stopped and let the animals drink. As they came out of the water it looked like it happened not very long before. She followed and some miles farther, coming to a rise, she stopped and got off from her horse. There were some bushes there and she tied Penny and walked on a ways to where she could see. There were the horses! There were 3 men, squatting on the ground, letting the horses rest. They had a little fire going and were making coffee, sitting at ease, talking. Apparently they were not expecting anyone to follow.

KING! She could see King. Looking around, she could see that the horses were gathered in a bunch and near the high bluffs where the river was narrow and deep. It was a steep place down into the river.

The men were seated, drinking coffee, and their horses were grazing and had worked a ways away from the men. King and the horses were closer to the river.

Dawn thinking: "If I call King will he come? He usually comes when I call him. Can I get him to follow me over and jump into the river? I think that he will! King won't want to be here, He will follow me!"

She went back and mounted Penny. "Penny, we have to be brave! But we can do this. We must! or we will lose our horses." She patted her neck, "Come on girl, let's go. Easy," she patted Penny's neck.

The men were noisy, talking and laughing and the metal clink with the coffee pot refilling their tin cups.

She rode slowly out into the open and unnoticed until she was near the horses and closer to the river.

There was a shout!

She yelled, "KING, KING! COME KING, COME KING!" She raced towards the horses until near them then turned and headed for the river, heading straight for it!

"COME KING, COME KING." She screamed. Looking over her shoulder, she could see King leading the rest of the horses, coming running, following her, racing for the river. Another look, the outlaw's horses were scattering, dragging reigns, running away, the other direction. She grinned at that but there was no time. Dawn, looking ahead towards the river, her hand patting Penny's neck, called:

"COME ON, PENNY, OVER WE GO, INTO THE RIVER. COME KING, FOLLOW US INTO THE RIVER! COME KING." They sailed over the edge. Dawn leaned back pulling Penny's head up to keep the balance on her rear quarters. They landed in the river with Penny landing well. Although the water was deep enough that they sank well up on Penny's side and she had to swim a ways. It hardly slowed her down as she continued across to a gravel bar and on down along the river. Looking back, Dawn could see the last of the horses plunging off the cliff and into the river. The men were not in sight.

"Come on you beautiful ones, let's go home." She called, slowing down, continued leading them down the river for several miles before they were able to climb out. The outlaws had not appeared. The horses followed her back to the pasture and entered without her urging them, she slipped off from Penny, closing the gate.

Dawn stood at the gate and King came to her and nuzzled his nose against her. She put her arms around his neck, patting him.

"I knew that you would follow me, King. I am so glad that you trust me that much. It would have been awful if we had lost you to those awful men." Tears stung her eyes.

Rosalea appeared at her side. "Where were you, Dawn? You were gone quite a while."

"I went looking for the horses, They were out of this pasture. But I found them."

The horses were dry, no sign of the wetting in the river. Dawn thought it better not to tell it all. No use adding any worry for her Mother. She had rescued the horses with no problems. They were home.

CHAPTER 17

John returned the next day with the report of the rustlers being caught. Joe Ames had bought a few young cows for them and their cattle would be brought to the ranch. He told of James' injuries and that he was to stay at the Ames ranch and would be there for several months, waiting for the broken leg to heal.

"Mrs. Ames insists that she will care for him. He must stay in bed for months with that leg propped up to heal. With the broken leg and the need that there be men to lift him and help with his care, there are several who will help to care for him at the Ames ranch."

John continued, "There are twenty five of the young cows that Ames bought for us. I will take money over to Joe Ames to pay him. Pete and Paul are bringing them on over."

The next day the cattle arrived and the men took them out to introduce them with the home herd.

Coming back to the house, Paul announced; "We are going to stick around and be sure that the new cows don't wander off. We will bunk in the barn."

"Pete, I can see that the snow is coming down lower and lower on the mountains," Rosalea said.

"It has been piling up, up there now for several weeks," Pete agreed.

"How soon can we expect snow down here? The weather is still nice but the temperature has been dropping a little." Rosalea said.

"We could get snow almost any day now. We could have had some before now. It is into November." Pete said.

He could tell by the look on her face, that Rosalea was worried.

"We could have a bad winter," Pete said. "I think that with James laid up for the winter, that Paul and I will come and spend the winter here. John and the two boys could have more than they can handle with the young cows and the rest of the cattle. Will you let us do that?"

"But aren't you needed at home?" Rosalea asked.

"Not really, Dad has a big crew, and they will hardly miss us. I think that we should be here."

"It would greatly relieve my mind if you would." Rosalea said.

"Then that is what we will do. We will go home and bring back our warm clothes and outfits. We will be back yet today," Paul declared.

After they left, Rosalea called to Rock, "Rock, with James unable to work and not even be here, Pete and Paul said that they want to help us and are coming back to spend the winter with us."

"That is good, Mam."

"Rock, please call me Rosalea."

"I can do that, gladly, if you want me to," he answered.

"I would like you to call me Rosalea, both you and Danny."

"And I want you and Danny both to call me Dawn," Dawn told them.

Danny grinned.

"Rock, the snow is lower and lower on the mountains and will soon be here. We didn't get the bunkhouse built. The barn is no place for any of you to sleep or spend any time unnecessarily there. You will all bunk in the house. Dawn will share my room, and Dawn's room can be for you and Danny or for Pete and Paul. The bunks in the living room for the other two. We will talk to them when they get here. So catch them before they can put their bedrolls in the barn and bring them in." Rosalea concluded.

Rock went out to do what chores that needed to be done. Danny saddled his horse and rode out to check on the cattle, reporting back that they were all together. Some were feeding and some lying down. The horses were near by. Rosalea thanked him and praised him for doing it.

"Just part of my job, Miss—uh—Rosalea" he grinned at remembering.

The men returned just as it was getting dark. Rock caught them in time to direct them to report to Rosalea.

"Rock said that we are to report to you?" Pete said.

Rosalea laughed, "Oh, not report. I didn't want you to think about bunking in the barn. Like I told Rock and Danny, the bunk house didn't get built and the barns are no place for any of you to bunk in. The weather will be getting colder. You will all sleep in the house. Dawn will be in my room. Her room can be for two of you, these bunks," she indicated the two bunks against the wall. "Two of you here. You can decide between you."

"Are you sure that you will have us all in here?"

"I insist," she answered.

"Paul and I will bunk in here and Rock and Danny have the room. Paul and I can see that the fire doesn't go out. I think that you may feel crowded with us all."

"Not at all. We will be glad. If we feel crowded we can go to our room. It is bad that you will be unable to do that, have some privacy. James wanted to get the bunkhouse built, but only got part of the logs cut and hauled in. The end of summer and fall has slipped by so quickly, so much has happened," Rosalea said. "Since there are so few of us, you will all be in the house."

"Rock and Danny, bring your beds in now too."

The men all brought their bedrolls in and put them on the bunks.

"I have coffee made, will you all sit at the table so that we may talk. Rock and Danny too," as they hesitated. "You are both part of our crew. We will be like a family," she said as an afterthought. She smiled at that thought. A big family including the Obeys.

Dawn brought cups and Rosalea poured coffee, Danny receiving his. Dawn passed a big pitcher of cream and the sugar around. That brought smiles.

Joining them at the table, Rosalea said "Dawn and I have never lived in a place like this and do not know just what to expect, but I think that you men will have much discomfort and maybe danger with the winter work. Will you tell us what to expect and advise us?" she continued, looking at Pete.

"We will need to see after the cattle and horses. I just wish that we had bigger loafing sheds to shelter the animals in. There is a canyon where there is some shelter. But the horses, I think that we will bring them in and keep them and the milk cow in. During the worse, we can keep the cattle and horses in the loafing shed," Pete told her.

"Last winter the weather did not get as bad as some. The loafing shed was big enough for the cattle and horses that we had. But this year it is not big enough for them all," Rock said, worry wrinkling his forehead.

"Is there any way that we can add to the loafing shed? Could the logs that are for the bunk house be used? I just wish that we had more of them. We do have some lumber and roofing," Rosalea said.

"Mam, Rosalea, we have quite a few more logs down, we just need to pull them in. There is more than enough to build a good sized bunk house and the lean/to that was to shelter the wood at the bunk house. We could use those logs for barns or shelter sheds. That would be more important now. There are a bunch of poles too," Rock said.

He added, "I should have been cutting more hay too. Last summer we borrowed a mower and rake from Joe Ames to cut hay. But with the more cattle we could use more hay this winter. With you folks bringing a mower and rake, I could cut hay if it just doesn't snow for a few days. There is a lot of the big tall grass hay standing off to the south near the garden. It should be enough. There are acres of it. I think that we will need more hay at the barn."

Paul said, "If the snow will just hold off a while, maybe we can get a lot done. We will bring the work horses in and put them to work."

"Rosalea, I think that we need to get together with John and his lads to make these plans. With all of us we will have a good crew." Pete said.

"Yes, we must do that. Let's go over and talk to them," Rosalea said.

They were soon gathered at John and Lilly's.

Rosalea said, "John, we have been talking and planning for the winter. I think that we have some ideas. Pete, can you men go ahead and plan what and how we will do."

The discussion continued with each one adding. Finally John spoke, "It is looking up for the winter now if we can get these things done before it snows. So, Pete, you and Paul have the most experience in this country, line us out, to get us started on what we each will do."

"Well, I hadn't thought to be 'ram rodding' this outfit," he grinned at them. "If we work together, it will work, and anyone with more ideas, let us know and we will talk about it. O.K.?" O.K.s all around.

"Rock, you said that you want to cut the hay, that we are going to need before winter is over. You go ahead," Pete continued.

"I will get started first thing in the morning," Rock said. "I should have been doing it by now."

"Good, when you need help, let me know. I can help you," Dawn said. "I can drive horses. Can I rake while you cut it down? You show me what to do and I will help. I will help wherever needed."

"I too," Rosalea said. "let me help."

"John, first thing, let's go haul in all of the logs and poles, have them ready to start building. With the five of us, that should not take us long. Maybe if it looks like not enough, maybe we could fall a few more trees."

"Yes, we could," John agreed. "There are still lots of trees out there. We were panning on a big lean/to shed for wood for the bunkhouse. We won't need the bunkhouse or wood shed this winter. There may be enough logs to add to the barn and loafing shed."

"Well, we know what will be the start for tomorrow," Pete concluded.

"I am going out first thing and bring all of the horses in," Danny spoke up.

And he did and had them in before breakfast was ready. The horse were given oats and were munching on hay when they went to harness them. Rock harnessed the team, hitched on the mower, headed out, starting to cut the hay.

Danny hitched up to a wagon, was going to haul in poles and he drove out to where the poles were. The men helped him to load the poles on the wagon and helped to unload them near the buildings. Danny hauled load, after load, sometimes having to wait a few minutes for help to load and unload the poles that were too heavy for him, but he handled many by himself.

The other men were soon dragging logs to near where they would be needed near the barn.

At her instance, Rosalea had convinced Rock that she and Dawn would wash up the dishes. "From now on, when you are busy at something, we will help by cooking and washing up."

"Only if Danny and I are needed elsewhere," he agreed.

"You are going to be cutting hay today, Dawn and I will cook dinner and supper." Rosalea said.

Rock, threw his hands in the air in resignation, grinning at her.

Dawn and Rosalea went to the garden and picked the last of the corn, beans carried them and the last of the squash into the cellar. They returned and dug the last of the potatoes, loading them in baskets and put them in the cellar too.

They had dinner ready at noon and Dawn ran out to Rock to call him come eat dinner and others came to eat as they returned with the logs. Log after log were accumulating near where they were going to built onto the barn. Danny's poles near by. Nightfall found that all of the logs and poles were hauled in. Rock returning from a great patch of hay down.

The sun set with a clear sky, "A promise of a clear day tomorrow," Rock declared. Supper time found the horses watered, rubbed down and feeding on hay in the small pasture. Lilly and her mother had helped to cook and they were all there. During the day, John's father had appointed himself as water boy and had carried the needed water and other things to help the women, even insisting on helping by washing vegetables and pealing potatoes.

"His health seams to be improving, He smiles and laughs a lot. His color is better and the lines even seem to have disappeared!" Rosalea thought as she noticed the old man's enthusiasm at the way he entered into the work. She was rejoicing, "This wonderful country is healing many things and Dad Obey isn't really very old! Thank you Lord! And won't it be good when my Dad and Mom come. The older ones will have friends here."

As they sat at supper, "Well, a lot done today," Pete said. "A good man's work from you too, Danny." Danny grinned at the praise.

"We got all of the logs and poles in. didn't we!" Danny grinned.

"We sure did! Now tomorrow, we start on building, another big job. How is the haying coming, Rock?"

"A good bit down. About as much left to cut. If it looks like we need more there is more about a mile away. What is down should be turned tomorrow."

"That sounds good, Rock," Pete said.

"The raking is for me to do," Dawn. "I promised my self before we came, that am going to learn to be a rancher."

"How are you going to manage having children,? pack your baby around on your back like the Indian women do," Paul asked her.

"Baby!" Dawn exclaimed. She turned towards Paul, "I will have to be married, have a husband before then. And that day is a long way off. I have a lot to learn to be a rancher before that day comes!" she declared.

Paul grinned, shook his head, but didn't say more. "I have my work cut out for me, if I am going to win that girl!" he thought. "Can I live up to it for her, be the rancher she will need and someday want?" The thought sobered him.

Pete looked at him and chuckled. But he knew that he, was going to have to prove himself to be the man that Rosalea needed.

Rosalea waved at Rock and Danny, "Get your beds ready. Danny needs to be in bed. Dawn and I are cleaning up."

John Senior and family were going home to their house. Men spread outside, checking on the animals and doing what needed done. Everyone was soon in bed.

Danny asleep before his head hit the pillow. Prayers were silently sent to their Lord.

Dawn remembered Paul's "Pack your baby around on your back? Me have a baby! Get Married! Some one? Some man! Is there a man out here?" Paul's blue eyes came to her mind. She could see those blue eyes! "Paul? Maybe Paul, some day. Not soon. I MUST learn to be a rancher first. A rancher's wife?" She fell asleep seeing those blue eyes.

The work progressed the next few days. The new barn was going to be built closer to the corrals and as big as the longest logs. It would be much bigger than the other barn. Logs were cut to length and fitted and the roof raised with some difficulty. Because of the length that they wanted for the barn roof, the logs were difficult to raise. Another pole had to be set in the middle to support the roof. Horses pulling, using ropes, raising the logs until they would fit into notched logs on the walls that were built first. Sometimes they thought they would never get the long logs for the roof in place, but finally the last log for the roof was in place. The poles for the shingles were easier and the roof only took two more days. Doors and shutters for over windows followed, the much bigger barn was built. A few more days seen the loafing shed enlarged. It was mostly enclosed, with an ell added, making a much larger and better sheltering area. It would shelter many animals.

Rock, with Dawn and Danny helping, hay was cut, turned to dry for a day and hauled in and piled into a hastily finished loft in the barn. More hay was stored in the loafing barns. Rock continued to cut hay, with Dawn and Danny turning it to dry a day or two and then piling it onto wagons and hauling it to the barns and the loafing shed. Some was stacked near by the best that they could and covered with some of the tarps.

Pete called a halt of Rock trying to find more hay to cut. "I think that will be enough for even a really bad winter, Rock. It is a wonderful job."

The cattle and horses were all in the pasture or near by, close enough to bring in, in a few minutes of storm warning. More fire wood was cut and stacked, much behind the stove and the attached wood shed was packed so full, they couldn't get in the outside door. It would have to be brought to the stove from inside the house. The path to the necessary was covered and enclosed. The same at the Obey's house. All made as safe and comfortable as possible.

Pete was satisfied that they had completed the work and the homes and animals would be protected for the winter the best that they could be. There would be chores every day but there were enough men to handle them. Even the milking. The women would not need to go out in the cold or stormy weather. And Pete was determined that they would not go out in the extreme cold and weather for any reason.

The morning came. As they sat at breakfast, Pete said, "Men and Ladies, we are as ready as we can get for winter to come. Still, I hope it will not be a bad one. What a great deal we have done! It is almost hard to believe what we have accomplished! We have a great crew here. I am proud of us all! May God bless us every one!" He raised his coffee cup, "I salute you all!" Cups were raised, "Salute" was raised all around. Danny, grinning with his coffee cup brimming with cream, was raised with the others. Pete touched his cup to Danny's. Faces had big smiles, some with tears sharing the smiles. Voices all around praising one then another.

Rosalea was beyond a voice, tears choking her throat. "My God, I thank you for all of these dear people," her heart sang.

A sudden thud!

"What was that?" Dawn, asked. The men grabbed jackets and went out to see, but when they opened the door, a blast of wind hit and howled around the house. Snow following it swirled into the house. Slamming the door shut, the men were back reaching for the heavy winter coats.

"Well, winter has come with a bang," Pete called out. "Come on men, lets get the animals in." He shrugged into a heavy coat hanging near the door, jamming on his hat on and tying it down with his bandana.

"You girls don't come out. We have enough men. Come on fellers, back to work, this is what we have been waiting for." He grinned, pulled on heavy gloves, waving the men to come as he went out. They were all soon in heavy winter clothes and out of the door. Even Danny was one of the first to go out.

The men found the animals huddled close to the fence and came when the men called to them and willingly went into the loafing shed. The horses anxiously pushed their way into barn stalls.

Rosalea and Dawn went to look out of the window and could see the snow driven in swirls past the house. As they stood watching, the visibility grew less and less. There was nothing but whiteness.

"How will they find the way back," Exclaimed Dawn.

A moment later and the door burst open, allowing a gust of wind that brought snow in with Danny, followed by Rock. Rock slammed the door shut and they were shaking snow off. Rock dropped bags of potatoes and a bag of dried beans. Danny had his arms full of bags of beets and carrots.

"Pete sent us back to bring in things from the cellar. Snow may cover up the cellar and we won't be able to get into it. John and the lads are helping with the cattle and horses."

They carried the bags to the back wall.

"Now to get water in. We will fill up everything." They took buckets and disappeared out the door again. After a few trips, everything available was full of water.

"What do we need to bring? coffee and anything else? Pete said that it may be days or even a week before we can get into the cellar."

"Oh, my! That long!" Rosalea exclaimed. "Let me think. A couple slabs of bacon and a bag of coffee. Another sack of flour and more salt and sugar. Why didn't I think of all this! There is a big bowl of butter. Our cow is not giving so much milk. We use most of the milk and cream. If you see something that we need or that you want, bring it."

They returned with several things, depositing them on shelves behind the stove.

While the men were getting the horses and cattle into shelter, Pete called to King, "Come King, come King," and King came to him. Pete took King and Penny and Pearl into the smaller barn and gave them grain as well as hay. Then moved the milk cow in there too.

"The water will freeze, and we will have to carry water to the animals," Pete told the men. Which they had to do every day for many days. It was part of what they had to do for the animals but there were several men for the different chores. Pete was careful to talk to and pet the two mares and King each time that he went out. King got so that he nickered when he seen Pete coming.

It was hours before the men came into the house. They looked more like snowmen than real men. They were crusted with snow. Slowly the coats and hats came off, snow was shaken off, and the coats and hats were carried to behind the stove to dry.

"Dawn and I will go into our room so that you men can change to dry, warm clothes," Rosalea told them, pulling chairs over near the stove. Dawn handed each one a towel. Rock was replenishing the fire. Danny was pulling off stiff ice crusted boots.

When the girls came back, the men were gathered around the stove and appeared to be pretty much exhausted.

"I have a rope here, we need to make a place to hang wet clothes to dry," Rosalea said.

Pete took the rope and soon had it stretched behind the stove and clothes hanging on it to dry.

"This will make it easier and quicker to get things dry," Rosalea said.

Pouring coffee, Rosalea asked "How did you ever find the house?"

"We tied a rope at the barn and around ourselves. When we found the house, we tied one end. Tying another here, and then went to John's house and tied it there. It is closer from John's to here than all the way to the barn. A rope from the barn to John's house might be buried in the snow. Now we are tied in touch."

"You took John home?"

"Yes. Couldn't take the risk of them getting lost in the snow."

"You are pretty wonderful men!" tears were in her eyes.

Pete grinned, "Didn't want to loose the help."

Dinner was soon on the table with lots of fresh coffee and warm bread just out of the oven. The lamp was lit and set on the table.

"It is so dark!" Dawn said.

"Pretty heavy clouds and lots of snow coming down and blowing around," Pete said.

Rosalea said, "Dawn, come help me."

They went to their room and Rosalea opened a large trunk. "These are all Tom's and James,' all of the extra that we bought. Let's give an outfit for each of the men."

"And I can share with Danny," Dawn said. "I have lots of extras. Even my boots are not much too big if he puts on a couple of pairs of the wool sox, which he will need with this cold weather. I have noticed that he is growing out of his cloths anyway."

"Three sets each for the men, and 4 pairs of sox each," Rosalea said.

"Three sets for Danny and 4 pairs of sox. I will still have a set for me," Dawn said as she counted them out and stacked them.

"Now to be sure they won't refuse." Rosalea said, picking the cloths up.

Rosalea carried the clothes to the table and stacked them in three piles.

She turned to the men, "When we were buying clothes, James suggested that we buy extras for enough for several years. At that time we did not know that we would have a store near by. But even so we could not get things for months. We have the extras of heavy warm winter clothes and we want you men to use them. I think that the sizes are close to your sizes." She separated out the stack for Rock. "We bought these for you Rock, James picked them out so if they don't fit, you will have to blame him," she laughed.

"Danny, these are for you. A bit big but you will soon grow into them. You need warm clothes or you can not go out side," Dawn said.

Danny came and looked at the clothes, "Even boots! And Sox!" his smile lit up his face. He turned and impulsively threw his arms around Dawn. She hugged him in return.

"These two stacks are for you, Pete and Paul. They are the same size. With the weather like this you will need dry clothes to change into after you come in. Please do not say no. It is little enough that we can do for you for all that you are doing for us."

"With weather like this, we will be very glad to have them. Danny hugged Dawn, now who do we hug?" Pete grinned and looked at first one then the other girl. "Or do we take our pick, like we did one day. No, I think that I need to hug each one of you wonderful ladies, to thank you!"

"Thanks are not necessary," Rosalea started to say, but he stepped to her and put his arms gently around her. He bent down and kissed the top of her head.

"Well don't me be a slacker in my thanks," Paul said as he reached Dawn and pulled her into his arms and kissed her cheek.

Dawn was startled, her mouth flying open and she was speechless, remembering that day and his intensely blue eyes.

"Her mouth is so tempting," Paul thought, "but this is moving too fast."

Pete followed Paul and hugged Dawn, kissing her hair on the top of her head.

Paul turned to Rosalea, hugging her and dared to kiss her cheek too.

The men stepped back and picking up the clothes took them to their bunks.

"Well, Danny," Rock said. "I guess that we need to be next in line to give homage to these wonderful ladies!" and he promptly hugged and kissed each. Danny followed, hugging them. He hid his face against Rosalea for a moment and there were tears when he turned to Dawn. Rock and Danny picked up their stack of clothes and took them to their room. Dawn and Rosalea fled to their room, they stood holding each other, shaken with the reaction of the men. Tears sparkled in their eyes. It was a little while before they came out.

"Dawn, remember the wool yarn that we brought? Let's knit some scarves. Some of the guys don't have a scarf. They need them to protect faces." They picked out yarn in red and bright blue. There were several colors.

"We can make several of each color." Which they did, knitting whenever they had time, giving the scarves as soon as one was completed. The men grinned their thanks, glad to have the added protection.

"Now men, we have a few books if you would like to read sometimes. Help your selves." Rosalea pointed to the shelves of books.

"Danny, Saraha Brooks is a teacher and she has some books. She sent a few home with me the last time I was there. A few that she thought that you maybe would like. Here is a Geography, that is interesting."

Danny turned red then pale. "Mam, Rosalea, I can't read very good. I only went to school for 2 years. I was just 9, then we left home and came west. We didn't have books with us, and then Mama and Dad died."

"Come on Danny," Dawn said, "I would like to read about Geography again. I love to read about places. That is one of the reasons why I came out west, because I wanted to see some of the places that I read about. And seeing is even better than reading about. This country out here is so very much greater and more wonderful than it was told about in any book. Don't you think so?"

Danny said, "I didn't read about it but my Dad had told us about this big country. It is really—a—like you said, it's wonderful here with you all."

She pulled him to the table and sat down with him, opening the big book. Paul sat down on the other side of him, "Do you mind if I look and listen," he asked.

"Welcome," Dawn said.

So many days went by with reading between times of caring for the animals. They took turns with the Geography book and a History book. Some days, when Dawn's voice grew tired, Paul would read for a while, sometimes taking time to explain something. On Sundays Rosalea read from the Bible.

One Sunday had been a hard day. The weather had moderated for a few days, then worsened again. The temperature dropped. Wind came again blowing swirling snow into every hole and opening in their clothing, under hats, nipping at ears and stinging their eyes to tears that froze on the scarves tied around faces. The chores outside done, the wind was howling around the eves and the continuous sound was grating on their nerves and on into the evening. It wasn't quite late enough for bedtime, even for Danny. Paul picked up the Bible,

"My voice is maybe a bit louder than Rosalea's, so I am going to read tonight." He opened the Bible and leafed through for a bit.

"This is one of my favorite places to read: It is in the book of John Chapter 3 and verse 16; 'For God so loved the world, that He gave His only begotten Son, that whosoever believeth in Him should not perish, but have everlasting life.' Verse 17; For God sent not his Son into the world to condemn the world; but that the world through Him might be saved." Paul closed the book, and sat thinking a moment. "It is like God is repeating the message to be sure that we understand. My Mother and

Dad had a Bible and read it to us. It has been read and read, until it is falling apart. They had us to learn that and many other places until we understood what it means."

"My Mama did too," Danny said softly. "I remember some that she helped me to learn. Mama talked to God like He was right there. I think that He was, even if I couldn't see Him." He stopped and sat staring into space, then he continued; "When those men came, Mama ran with me and put me in some bushes and told me to be very quiet and lay still. She prayed and said, 'God protect my dear little son and help him to grow up to be a good God loving man.' She pulled some grass and leaves and put them over me. But I sat up and watched her as she ran back to Dad and she picked up a rifle and started shooting. I got real scared and pulled the grass and stuff over me. It was awfully noisy and I covered my ears and laid there for a long time. After a while it wasn't so noisy but I was still scared so I laid real quiet. It got dark and Mama and Dad didn't come after me. It was awful dark and I didn't know how to find them. I laid there and fell asleep." Tears were running down his face.

"When I woke up I moved the grass off from my face and looked but I couldn't see any one. So I went to find Mama and Dad. They were both dead. Our horses were gone. The wagon was tipped over and I couldn't find any food but some flour. I tried to eat it but it was too dry. I got some water and put some flour in the water but I couldn't make a fire to cook it. I was awfully hungry so I ate it anyway." He stopped and rubbed the tears from his face. Then he looked up at Paul, "I guess God did look after me, 'cause the next day Rock came and took me away with him. I have been with him since. I guess God had Rock come to find me." Danny turned and looked at Rock, "He's my good friend. He teaches me lots of things, to help me grow up to be a good man, like Mama said. I think that I love God, he sure is taking good care of me." A smile spread across his face, "He even brought me here with all of you,"

Tears were slipping down Rosalea and Dawn's faces.

Paul was blinking as he reached and ruffled Danny's hair. "God surely takes care of us many times. He leads us into right ways if we will go His way."

"Time for some hot cocoa," Rock said, as he stood up to hide the tears that were running down his face. "Thank you Rosalea for bringing cocoa." Rock made a big kettle of hot cocoa, made with milk and cream floating on top. It was enjoyed by all, soothing the tight throats, returning smiles to faces.

Later as he lay in bed, Rock was thinking, "Oh God, did you bring me to help this dear boy? Then I thank you. I am so sorry that his Mama and Dad died. I couldn't have stopped that. I wish that I could have. I am the one who is the better for what happened after that, In finding Danny. His Mama has to be proud of him. He is a fine boy, and has the makings of the good man his Mama prayed for. He is a blessing in our lives."

In the night Rosalea thought about the evening. "God is binding us together with friendship that is almost like family. Little Danny! And Rock! Even Pete and Paul! They are good men. I think that Danny is right, God brought them to help us through this bad winter! What would we have done without them."

Her thoughts turned to Tom, and she cried quietly, not to wake Dawn. Then a thought startled her! Did God bring Pete to help her with the loss of Tom. Then she remembered the promise that Tom had made her promise, to make a new life here in the new land. Was Pete to be a part of the new life? She fell asleep trying to think about that. Pete's blue eyes haunted her dreams.

Finally the weather changed. Spring was slow in coming but the temperature grew warmer. The snow slowly melted.

Then a day came and they could see green grass beginning to grow. There were remnants of snow drifts in places, but spring was coming.

Pete and Paul stood leaning on the fence, watching the cows and horses moving out of the corrals to seek the green grass. There was still hay stacked and they had put some in the corrals, but the animals were wanting to forage for the green grass.

At last Pete spoke, "This has been a hard winter, and we have had many like this one over the years. Another year with the increase of the herds, there will be no way that the cattle can be cared for here like we did this winter."

"What can we do? Will they have to keep the herd as small as these? Sell the calves?" Paul asked.

"Out where the trees were cut, may be a sheltered area big enough to serve as winter shelter," Pete said.

"Let's ride out there and have a look," Paul said.

They topped the ridge and could see where the trees had been cut.

"Look Paul, this place is a valley with a south facing. See, there is no snow down here anymore."

"And there is a lot of last years grass left. A lot of grass," Paul said.

"And the new grass is 8-10 inches high already."

"The hills are off to the west, north and clear around to the east towards the south, making a big bowl, facing the south. The hills are high enough that it will be protected from the north and north/west winds here. It should be warmer down in this valley, a perfect place to winter the animals," Pete declared.

"It looks like just what they will need," Paul said. "I wonder if James and John knows this about this sheltered valley."

"If not, we need to bring John and Rosalea and Dawn here and see this," Pete said.

Taking Rosalea, Dawn, and Rock and Danny, they went to talk to John, he said, "James and I had talked about that valley and had almost decided to build there, but we thought that the little creek would not be enough water for all of our needs. It runs year around but not a lot of water."

"And the summers get pretty warm there," Rock added. "We talked about maybe building a cabin and place for horses and a couple or 3 guys sometimes stay there in the winter with the herd after the herd got bigger."

"I think that the herd is going to be too big for another winter like this last one here at the ranch buildings," John said. "I think that we will have the herd in that valley this coming winter. We will plan and prepare for that."

"How about the smaller barn being turned into a bunkhouse?" Pete asked. "We used it for part of the animals but another year, it won't be needed."

"It is a really good and warm building. It is far enough away from the big barn. I think that is what to do with it," John said.

"I am going to go get James," John said. "It is long past time for him to be home. He should be here."

"Danny and I will go with you," Rock said, grinning. "We will take the wagon and he can ride in the wagon."

"Rosalea, the weather is warm enough, we will move out to the hay, until we get the bunkhouse fixed," Pete and Paul took their bedrolls out to the hay.

There wasn't much hay in the soon to be bunkhouse and they hauled it out, cleaned out the straw bedding, then took a broom and swept down the walls and the dirt floor. There were left over pieces of logs, and they put them down for a sub floor.

James came limping, leaning on a hand build crutch. They greeted him: "Welcome home. You are just in time to advise us. We are making this into the bunk house."

"It will make a good one!" James said.

"Oh my! What a lot you fellows have done! And me laying around while all of this was being done." James stood looking around.

"How can I advise you! You have done pretty great so far."

"Well, we have pieces of logs down for a floor, is there anything that we can use to finish the floor?" Pete asked.

"Under that tarp is a stack of flooring. There should a lot more than needed for this," James said. "And lumber to make several bunk beds for the bunkhouse too."

"Danny, if you will take care of the horses, I will help here." Rock said.

They soon had the floor down.

Rosalea and Dawn had watched but soon urged James to go to the house and sit down.

"I haven't been outside much yet, and I get tired easily," James confessed. "Too many weeks laying around waiting for this leg to heal. Now I will walk around and gain some strength."

"It is good to have you home, Uncle James," Dawn told him and hugging him.

"We have missed you but it was probably better for you, that you were not here during this tough winter," Rosalea said. "I don't know how we could have managed without Pete and Paul. It would have really hard for John, Rock and the boys. They wouldn't let Dawn and I hardly out the door."

A few days and the bunkhouse was finished, with a stove installed too.

They were sitting around the table, supper over, coffee cups refilled. Each seemed to be lost in thoughts.

Pete's thoughts; "I want to marry this lady. Shall I take her home to TXT or shall I ask about joining in a partnership here? I could bring a bunch of cattle. Should I ask her now—or wait until fall? Maybe wait. What is Paul going to do about Dawn? He may not want to wait until fall. But Dawn? She may not want to marry him. I think that Paul and I had better go home to the TXT for a while."

Rosalea spoke, "Pete, I was telling James how much we needed you and Paul this winter. I don't know how we would have managed without you. It would have been really hard for Rock and John and the boys. We owe you so very much! How can we ever repay you?"

"No pay, please, of any kind. Don't think of that. If we had been at home, we wouldn't have had much to do. And Dad has a big crew. The winters get so bad, that we fight over who gets to do what, just for something to do," he laughed. "So you see, being here was a good thing for us, giving us something to do and keeping us learning to be ranchers," he grinned at her.

"That is for sure," Paul said. "And kept us out of mischief. We mighta got in fights just to have something to do."

"But now we do need to go home. The work with the cattle at the TXT starts now and we will be busy all summer and into the fall."

"Will you need help with branding, James?" Paul asked. "We can come help you then."

James answered; "I should be getting around pretty good by then and we can manage with what cattle we have this year. Another year or two we may need to have a couple more guys. But this year we should be able to do it."

"We got to use the new bunkhouse before we left, anyway," Paul said. "I am looking forward to coming back and using it again."

"You will always be welcome here any time you will come." Dawn said.

"Yup! That's for sure. I like you guys." Danny said. "It feels like you belong here with us. Part of our family."

Rosalea thought, "that is so! Like we are family!"

"But now you are going home?" is what she said.

"Yes," Pete said, "Now we go home." 'God, I am going to miss her, them all,' he thought.

"We will head out in the morning, unless there is something that we can do?"

"It looks like you fellows have everything in order. And John and the boys and Rock and Danny will be here," James said. "We can never thank you enough for all that you have done."

The next morning they watched the two young men ride away.

"Well, it is time for us to start our garden!" Rosalea said.

"I am going to start plowing," Rock said. "Come help me to plan the garden, Rosalea."

"I am going to get the horses," Danny said.

"I will go with you," Dawn said.

Penny and Pearl were the only horses in.

"You ride Penny and I will ride Pearl," Dawn told Danny.

They soon could see the horses and Dawn called, "KING!! KING!! COME KING!! COME KING!" He lifted his head and nickered, shook his head up and down and trotted to her. She pulled a carrot out of a pocket for him.

"You didn't forget, did you King! And it has been a while since I have called you."

They separated out a team of the work horses and took home. King followed them home.

"Some one is going to ride you King," Dawn told him as she put him in the corral. "You have been loafing around long enough," she laughed.

Rock soon had horses harnessed and was plowing the garden.

"King!" Rosalea called to him. He came to her. "We are going for a ride," she told him and he was soon saddled and they headed out. She rode out to the valley that they had talked about for winter pasture. She rode far down in the valley and found where a spring bubbled out of the rocks and the small stream was borne. She got off and cupped her hand and tasted the water.

"It is good, King!" He tasted the water, then drank more. She laughed, "It is good hunh and so cold!"

She looked around, "This is where they may build a winter cabin. It is beautiful here. Quiet and peaceful. Maybe it won't be in the winter when a storm hits. But it will be sheltered here. It is more sheltered here than the up at the ranch buildings."

She rode out of the valley and on out towards the north a ways. Coming out on a rise, she stopped to look.

"I have never been this far before." She was looking down into a river deeply imbedded in a vast canyon. She could see the canyon with the river wondered off to the northeast for a long ways. On to the north, mountains raised their glacier covered heads.

"Oh what big, beautiful country! It is almost unbelievable! So—much!" She sat, trying to see everything. "It is awesome!" She exclaimed at last. King stood looking and suddenly turned his head a bit and nickered.

"What? What do you see King." Then she seen something moving. It was a long ways off, Rosalea thought, 2 or 3 miles. "That ridge—Horses!—A bunch of horses—No riders—wild horses? They are going the other way. Well, King, if those are wild horses, we don't want anything to do with them. There is probably a stallion, and he won't like us. Let's go home King!" Turning she put him to a mile eating gallop.

She gave him a good rubdown before she turned him into the corral. She stood petting him. "It was a good ride, wasn't it King. I have needed this time today. Thank you, King. We will do it again soon."

Although the Ogerly men were missed at the Larson/Obey ranch, they would be busy. The garden was tilled and planted and a few yards of strips each of wheat and oats and in a few weeks, beans, carrots and beets would be planted. A little, later corn and potatoes. They would plant enough that there would be plenty to see them through the winter and seeds left to plant for another year. This is as it would always be.

The weather was warm and the garden grew quite rapidly. Flower seeds of several varieties were planted around the house. There would soon be colors blooming.

There were new calves, of the milk cows and beef cows, increasing the herds. The hens each soon had a brood of chicks, the rooster parading around the yard, proudly crowing every few minutes, as though bragging about the baby chicks. Soon Spring blossomed into summer.

James was building two more rooms onto the house. Plans were made for the cabin that they would build down in the winter pasture area.

Everyone was busy, yet there was a feeling of waiting. Rosalea and Dawn talked about it and wondered. They hadn't heard from Pete and Paul but they knew that Pete had said that they would be very busy. And the TXT ranch was 50 miles away. They wouldn't have time to come by for some time.

Rosalea and Dawn rode almost every day, sometimes together, sometimes alone. They didn't ride far, but wanting to ride and using to exercise the horses as a reason to ride many days. They still wore the boy clothes most of the time, only putting on dresses on Sundays riding in the wagon, going in to church.

One of the milk cows was going to have a calf and one Sunday morning it looked like this was the day. John, James, Rock and the boys had gone to the Ames ranch to help there for a few days. Rosalea and Dawn and the Obeys were going to go to church, but when Rosalea went to check on the cow, she decided to stay home.

"I will saddle King and come on later and we can spend the afternoon with them in town," so she sent them on.

The calf was soon born and Rosalea watched it until it was nursing. King nickered at her and he was coming over to her. She took a pitch fork full of hay and tossed over the top rail into the corral and as she pulled the fork back it drug the top rail and the rail fell down. King jumped and turned around and snorted. He stomped his feet and snorted again. Rosalea turned to see what King was looking at. A man was just stepping off his horse and coming towards her, he threw the gate of the corral down. "Watch her, men. Don't let her get away," he yelled.

"King," she reached for him and he came to her. She grabbed a handful of mane and leaped on him. "Let's go King," she urged him over the bottom rail and out into a run. "Can I ride and control King without saddle or bridle?" she wondered.

"Head her off," the man yelled, "don't let her go to town. Catch her!"

Rosalea leaned over Kings neck. "Come on King! Let's go King, Go!"

King galloped out past the barns to head for town but there were two riders there. She put her hand on the side of King's neck, turning him away from them, more to the northwest. The men were close.

"Go King Go!" she cried. He leaped into a full run. Go to the Ames ranch, she thought. But the two men on her left had good horses and she couldn't get ahead of them far enough to turn to the Ames ranch. On they raced. She didn't know what happened to the man at the corral. She thought that there was a couple more men in the yard, all behind her now she believed. Five men chasing her, maybe 6.

"Oh, God! help me. Can I get past them to get to the Ames ranch?" She didn't seem to be pulling away from those on her left. If she couldn't soon, they would catch her when she turned that way. Mile after mile they raced and they kept abreast of her. She soon knew that she must turn now to the Ames ranch.

"They are still there! Can't get past them! Keep going on to the TXT, the Ogerly ranch 40 more miles! But I am lighter and with no saddle, King is carrying less weight! Can I stay on that far?"

She tried to look behind her, yes she could see men racing, following.

"My only hope the Ogerly ranch! But I don't know where it is! 40 more miles! If we can just keep a steady pace for a while, we may have a chance."

Her thoughts had raced. She continued to lean over King's neck, keeping down to cut the wind desistance. Mile after mile they raced. Then she could see that the two men on her left were slowly falling behind. When they were about a half mile behind, she raised up a bit as a signal for King to slow. He did and she checked the other men behind her, it looked like they had dropped behind some too.

"Good boy King," she patted him. "But we have a long way to go yet." She let him slow into a pacing trot but then she could see the men beating their horses into a run again.

"Pick it up a bit, King. Let's go." He went into a smooth gallop, faster, but not racing. The men began to gain slowly. "But they are whipping their horses and they could tire quicker than King," she thought. Soon she saw that the men were slowing to a trot. The horses behind her were quite a ways back. She slowed King to a walk. He took a deep breath and snorted.

"Good boy King!" She could see the men pull their horses to a walk too.

"Five minutes and then we go again. Can't let them get rested. I know that we are lighter, and you are in good shape."

Suddenly something hit her arm from behind, then the sound, a shot!

"Oh God They are shooting at us! Oh God, don't let them hit King! Come on King! Go King! Go!"

He leaped into a racing run again. How far, she wondered. It seems like hours. Another shot, the bullet hit the ground just to her left.

"Go King Go" She screamed. "Go find Pete, find Pete, King, find Pete," King leveled out and seemed to fly low to the ground. The wind whipped his mane past her face where she bent her head down, and she couldn't see any more. It seemed that time stood still and they were stuck there, stuck racing and racing, that time went on and on. "I have to hang on,—hang—on. Find Pete, King, Find Pete!" on they raced, how long? A long time racing! Then suddenly King broke his stride and he slowly came to a stop. Rosalea raised her head. They were in among a bunch of riders. The roar continued in her ears—it was still there. But someone was shouting her name.

"Rose—Rosalea!"

"King, come King" some one was calling King!

There was Pete, along side of her lifting her off from King, into his arms.

"Rosalea, what is going on?"

"Men chasing King."

"Men chasing you? How many men chasing you?"

"Six,—they shot at us."

"Oh God, she's bleeding!" that was Pete.

"who's bleeding?—

"Pete! Hang onto me!"

"We are going after them!" was that Paul shouting? Sounds like Paul's voice.

"Tim, put King in the barn. Take care of him." That's Pete's voice.

She lifted her head, "Pete?—I might fall off. Oh somebody? Tim? Tim has King. Pete, King brought me, we ran—we—got away—didn't we? We found you, but I don't know where you are."

"We ran so fast,—King ran so far so fast,"

"Yes, King brought you to me and I've got you. I'm holding you."

"Pete, watch out, those men have guns. They shot at us with a rifle. We were too far for pistols, but rifle almost hit us. Oh be sure about King, that he didn't get hit."

"Rose—hold still—Let me hold you, Rose. Tim is taking care of King. I am going to take care of you. I am going to take you in the house—"

"House? We found you!"

"Yes you found me and King is alright."

She turned her face against his chest, her head nestled into the hollow of his shoulder, next to his heart, and she closed her eyes.

"Rose? Rose?"

"I'm alright now. I'm gonna hang on and stay right here. I'm so—tired."

"Mom?" Pete's voice?

"sooo—tired—hang—on. Hang onto a new life? Promised new life. Pete? Hang on—"

"I've got you, Rose, I'm holding you."

"holding me? Pete?"

"Yes, Sweet Heart, I'm holding you!"

(earlier, back to Pete at TXT ranch)

The long job of hunting Cattle out of the brush filled canyons had taken time. And then to haze them up out into the open on the green grass. Pete had come out into the open and sat looking at the cattle. The cattle were spreading out over the rolling prairie, cattle in sight, spreading out everywhere. Miles and miles of cattle. His Dad rode up.

"Quite a herd, Dad. How many do you think?" Pete asked.

"There are probably some we didn't find. This herd, maybe 20,000 head. We need to sell a bunch this fall."

They sat for a while, watching more cattle coming up. Then Tony Ogerly said, "I thought that you would bring a wife home with you when you came. What happened?"

"I didn't ask her. She maybe a couple years older than I. Would she have anything to do with a guy like me?"

"She would be lucky to get a guy like you. Didn't you pretty much prove yourself to her during the winter?"

"Yes, I think so. It was a pretty busy time and she was really glad that we were there and thanked us when we left. It was a good thing that we were there. The winter storms were pretty bad. Paul talked like he was going back after Dawn." Pete grinned.

"So, are you going to go get her?"

"Can I bring her here?"

"Why not. This is a big ranch. It should support a half dozen families and a couple dozen kids."

"Kids!—She might say no, you know!"

"Won't happen, Son. Look in the mirror."

"Alright! I will go get her. If she will just say yes."

They turned and headed for the ranch house. The whole crew were soon gathered in the yard, all still mounted.

"Rider coming!" some one called. "Coming hell bent for election."

The horse and rider were soon in their midst.

"It's King, and Rose!"

"Rose! Rosalea!"

"King! Come King!" Pete called to him. King came close, brushing against his leg and against his horse, close enough that Pete could reach out and take Rosalea off from King, lifting her in his arms.

"Tim, take care of King."

"We are going after those men that were chasing Rosalea," Paul shouted. "Come on men. Their horses should be pretty tired out and we can catch them."

Pete rode over to the porch. "Dad, help me to get down with her."

"Mom?'

"In here, Pete. I think that she is asleep. The dear must be tuckered out after that ride. Pull her boots off, Pete. Let's get her undressed, out of these dusty clothes."

A little later, the small wound in her arm bandaged, Mom was brushing the girls hair.

"What beautiful hair! Look at this, Pete!"

"I know. And Dawn's is just like it."

"Dawn?"

"Her daughter Dawn."

"Let's go let her sleep."

"NO," she reached out and grasped Pete's arm and pulled him to her. She raised up and leaned against his shoulder. "Hold me, I don't want to fall off." Her eyes had not opened.

"I'm holding you, Rose, you won't fall." He gathered her against his chest and settled there against the head of the bed, to hold her until she would wake.

After a bit, Pete prayed, "Thank you God, that King brought her to me." What else he prayed?

Paul and the rest of the TXT crew caught up with the now fleeing outlaws to soon be met by a group of other riders coming. That group of riders proved out to be Texas Rangers.

"We have been tracking this bunch from Abilene. We lost their tracks a couple weeks ago and just found tracks yesterday. They have been cattle thieves and horse thieves. They have killed 20 or 30 men. They will hang." The Ranger assured them.

"Can you hang them here?" Paul asked. "They shot at and wounded one of our women."

"I wish that we could, but Texas Rangers enforce the laws. So back to Abilene. Thank you men for helping catch them."

"I am going on to find Dawn and the rest, they may not know what happened to Rosalea," Paul told his riders. They followed him, but when they reached the Obey/Larson ranch, no one was there. They headed for Culbert's store.

As they rode into the yard, everyone came out.

"Paul!" Dawn cried, "You here, is something wrong?"

"Do you know where Rosalea is?" Paul asked.

"At home, one of the cows was calving, and she stayed, but she said that she would ride King over as soon as she could come. She hasn't come yet."

"And everyone else is here and alright?"

"Yes! You scare me, Paul, Is something wrong?"

"Not any more." And he told them all that had happened.

"King ran all the way to the TXT, he brought Rosalea to Pete. He took her right to Pete. And Rosalea is at the TXT with Pete. She is pretty well tuckered out, and hopefully sleeping." Paul concluded.

"Can you come back with me?" Paul asked.

"But there is only Lilly, Grandpa and Gramma Obey and I at our ranch. James and John, all of the men and the boys are at the Ames ranch."

Paul slapped his gloves against his leg. "Dd-d-d! And Rosalea was alone out there when that bunch came. Thank God for King or your Mother would have gone through hell and probably died—or killed herself. One thing for sure, the Obey/

Larson men must take better care of their women if the want to keep them. Rock and Danny went with them?"

"Yes."

"If Rock and Danny had been at the ranch and armed, maybe they could have run those men off. These people have to realize that there may at any time be outlaws coming by. There is always an outlaw element happening on the frontier. There are those who don't want to work, they just want to take and take what ever and where ever that they can."

Dawn was pale. "We have been told to always wear a gun," she whispered.

"Where is your gun?" Paul pointed to where it should have been hanging around her waist.

"At home."

"Why? And how many times have you been caught in danger without it? You have. Haven't you?"

"Yes!"

"And still your forget. At this rate, you may never live to learn to be the rancher, that you talked about becoming."

Dawn covered her face with her hands and burst into tears.

"Oh God! Dawn!" Paul pulled her into his arms, holding her tight. She clung to him and continued to cry.

"Dawn," Paul took her by the shoulders and held her back, "Look at me. Stop crying. Now. Marry me and I will take you to the TXT and you will never be left alone anywhere at anytime. If I am not with you, there is a group always at the ranch. You and Rosalea will be protected."

"What if we go riding alone?"

"You won't."

"We do. We will."

"You won't. No one will let you have a horse. You will ride with me or someone who is armed with pistol and rifle. Rosalea will ride with Pete."

"Is she going to stay there?"

"Pete will never let her go alone. If she comes back here, he will come with her."

"He is gong to stay with her?"

"She is going to stay with him. He is going to marry her."

"Marry!—You said—marry you!" she whispered, remembering.

"Yes. I said; Marry me. Now. Today. That man," pointing, "Jonathan Brooks can and will marry us. Now. Today." Paul repeated. He still held her by her arms, making her to look into his face. Then he smiled.

"I am only 18!"

"Old enough. My mother was only 16 and she has been married a few years and 8 children."

"Ooohhh"

"I can't—I WON'T leave you here."

"But it is our ranch, John and James and Mom and my ranch." She protested.

"It is a young ranch. Right now, it is understaffed, unprotected. Remember last winter? Where would have you been without Pete and I?"

"I know. We maybe would have died!" she cried.

"Could have. If you father had lived, maybe it would have been different. Let's let James and John get the help from the Ames ranch and develop the ranch. The Ames ranch is closer and they already work together. James will be marrying one of the Ames girls and Ames will never let her go without seeing that this ranch is fortified and running protected. The young Obeys will marry and have families. Given time, this will be a great ranch. They do not need you. Pete and I do. The TXT needs you. Your mother, Rosalea, will NOT be coming back here. Pete will not let her come back here. Pete and I fell in love with you two and have decided that you will marry us. Marry me, Dawn, and come home to the TXT with me. Marry me today, now. Now?"

He was still holding her arms, making her look up into his eyes.

She stood looking into his eyes, those compelling eyes that showed the love that he had for her. She reached her arms up to his shoulders and slid them around his neck and she melted against his chest. His arms went around her, gathering her against him.

"Is that yes?' he whispered against her ear!

"Yes!" she whispered.

He held her back, "Yes?" looking into her eyes.

"YES" she said, looking up at him. She was smiling through tears that overflowed her eyes.

Paul turned to the others, "She said YES, she said yes!"

"We heard her, Paul," Jonathan assured him.

"Now? Dawn, now? Dawn? Now today?"

"Well, yes, now—today—but let me think a minute. Can I go get into a dress to get married in?"

"Yes, you can go get a dress."

"I will go with you, Dawn, and help you," Lilly Obey said.

"You will come back here to get married won't you?" Jonathan asked.

"Yes, can we get married in the church?" Dawn asked.

"Yes!" was echoed by Jonathan and Paul.

At the ranch, Lilly said, "you need to take your things and your mother's things and take them to her. Paul said that Pete won't let her come back here. We will pack your things and her things."

The women packed the things into the big chests and they were put into the wagon that sat waiting, the same wagon that they had used earlier to go for Sunday. Back in town, Saraha

Brooks had gathered a few flowers for Dawn and put a few in her hair as well.

It was a simple ceremony, witnessed by all, including the riders who had came with Paul. The cowboys, Grinning, each clamed their right to kiss the bride. There was no doubt that Dawn and Paul were married after all of the well-wishes and blessings.

"Paul," Will Culbert called," I know that you are married and want to head for the TXT but it is nearly dark, why not wait until morning to start the long trip? You and Dawn can have a room in Molly Craft's. The rest can bunk around. Or even go back out to Obey/Larson bunkhouse. Some one needs to go out and milk the cow anyway. I can do that."

The older Obeys and Lilly would be staying in town until John Obey and James Larson and crew returned. Paul had talked with Will Culbert and they had agreed that the older couple and Lilly should stay in town, not go back out to the ranch. They would bring the milk cow to town, and there they would stay for some time.

When the group with the wagon left the next morning, the baby calf rode in the back of the wagon, the new mama and another cow went with them. A basket with chickens was tied on the side of the wagon. Another wagon, driven by Jonathan Brooks, carrying Lilly Obey, and Saraha Brooks and leading the milk breed bull, all went with them. The other milk cows would be kept in town.

It would be after noon before they reached the TXT ranch.

Some time in the night Rosalea had slid down on the pillow and slept. Pete unwilling to leave her if she would rouse and wake alone, he had stayed. Whether awake or asleep when he settled his head on the pillow near her, there he slept.

Rosalea woke slowly, wondering? Her cheek was resting on something warm? She didn't move, slowly opening her eyes. Where was she? Close, she could see blue flannel? Blue flannel shirt? Under her face? Her arm was across that blue flannel shirt! Her head was resting on that blue flannel shirt!! Who's? Pete!! She was in his arms. She could feel his arms holding her! Memory flooded back, of the awful wild race on King trying to escape from men chasing her and King! That race to find Pete at the TXT. They had made it! King had taken her to Pete! She had slept on Pete's chest! In his arms. This then was the new life? I can't go back! Wicked men trying to capture me! I would die. I am here with Pete. He held me! He is still holding me! Can I stay here? Will Pete want me—here? A longing filled her, a longing to belong here, here in Pete's arms. The new life! She moved a bit at that thought. Pete woke and was looking at her. They sat up, looking at each other.

"Good morning Sweet Heart! Did you get your sleep out?"

"Pete! I am here!"

"Yes, you are, you are here, here with me. And here you stay. Someone may come after you, but King brought you to me, and I am going to keep you. Keep you here with me. Here on the TXT. Dad said that this ranch is big enough for several families and here we will stay and live. We are going to be married and live here."

"A new life!" she whispered.

"Yes, a new life, here with me."

Pete's mother stepped in, "Well, are you two awake and ready for something to eat? Come along Rosalea, let's get you cleaned up a bit and you must eat."

She had found clothes for Rosalea and helped her to dress.

Tony Ogerly joined them and had coffee while they ate.

"I am glad to welcome you to the TXT ranch," he said as he extended his hand to her.

"How are you this morning Rosalea? Are you recovered from that wild race?"

"Yes, I think so. It really was a wild race! King is a great horse and outran all of the other horses and brought me here. Is King alright?"

"Yes he is. He has been in the barn and rubbed down and watered and fed. He is a beautiful animal. I think that he may be looking for you, he looks at everyone who goes into the barn."

"OH! I want to go see him!"

"As soon as you have eaten, we will go out and see him," Pete told her.

Pete's Mom brought 3 apples to her, "Give him a treat from me," she said, handing her the apples.

"He will be happy with these!" Rosalea exclaimed.

As they entered the barn, King turned to see her and nickered and stomped his foot.

Rosalea put her arms around his neck and her face against him.

"King! King!," she cried into his neck. "You dear, wonderful horse! I owe you my life! You ran all that long way with me! You brought me here to Pete! You found him! You found Pete!"

Pete stood beside her, petting the King. A soft nicker as King looked at Pete.

"I think that King understands everything that you say to him," Pete said.

"Of course he does! He is a wonderful horse!"

"I agree with that! He sure proved that in taking care of you and that long hard race!"

She put the apples on her hand, offering them to him.

"A present for you from a very dear lady, King. You must get to know her too."

King ate the apples, slowly as if he was savoring each bite.

Tim entered the barn, "I think that he has been waiting for you, to be sure that you are here somewhere. He looks at the door whenever anyone comes into the barn. He is a wonderful horse, Rosalea."

"He is alright, isn't he? He didn't get hit when we were shot at did he?"

"No, he is in good shape after that long hard race. No harm anywhere that I can see," Tim told her. "I have rubbed him down several times and looked him over real good. I have checked his legs too. He lets me lift his feet to check his hooves. He seems to be sound everywhere."

"Are you going to keep King, Rosalea, or do you need to return him to James?" Pete asked her.

"I am going to keep him! He is mine! However could I give him up." She clung to his neck. "All the way across the prairie he would come when Dawn and I called him. He would lead the other horses to us."

"Pete, when those men came after me, King, laid he ears back and snorted at the man. He knew that he was a bad man and didn't like him to be there. That is why I knew to jump on King and run away," Rosalea said.

"Good man King, I sure am glad that you took such good care of Rosalea, and brought her to me." Pete stood patting the horse.

"I think that we will take King out to the little pasture out here near the barn," Tim said. "Maybe he will like it. Come on King." Tim lead him out of the barn to the pasture. King turned and came to the fence, looking at Rosalea.

"It is alright King, go enjoy a little more room," Rosalea patted his neck. "Go, King. I will be here somewhere. I am not leaving you."

King went and looked around and picked out a place to lay down and roll. He got up and lay down and rolled again. Then he stood and shook himself. Then looked for some green grass to munch on.

"He seems to be content," Pete laughed.

"Someone's coming," someone called as they walked back towards the house.

"Two wagons, coming with our TXT outfit," big Tony Ogerly said, reaching out to stop one of the teams.

Dawn jumped down from the wagon, "Mama! I'm here too," she cried as she ran to her mother.

"Mama, I am married to Paul. He said that you will marry Pete?"

"What? You married! To Paul?"

"Yes, Mama. Married to Paul. He brought me and he brought Jonathan Brooks to marry you and Pete. Paul said that we, you and I, aren't going back to the Larson/Obey ranch. We are going to live here on the TXT as the wives of Paul and Pete. It is a big ranch and Tony Ogerly says that is the way it is going to be."

Tony Ogerly, laughed and said, "That is what I said, that is the way it is going to be. We need you women and the families that we will have on this big old ranch. My sons need wives and children. You women are here to stay."

Rosalea looked up at Pete, "You want to marry me?"

"Yes, Rosalea, I want to marry you. Will you marry me?"

She stood looking up at him. "Pete! Are you sure that you want to marry me?"

"I am very sure. How about you, do you want to marry me?'

Rosalea's eyes filled with tears that took that moment to run over and run down her cheeks past her joy filled smile. Her hands reached out to him and he pulled her into his arms to kiss away the tears, at last finding her lips.

"Oh, Pete," she whispered.

"Is that Yes, Yes that you will marry me, Rosalea." He asked.

"Oh! Yes, Pete, Yes!"

"She said Yes!" Pete shouted.

"We heard," Tony Ogerly said.

"I came to perform that very thing for you," Jonathan Brooks said, laughing.

"Mama, we brought our clothes and things. Let's go find you a dress to be married in." Dawn told her.

King had been watching since the wagons had arrived. He nickered several times, the stomped his feet and nickered again. Then he whistled and turned and ran to the far side of the pasture. He turned and raced across the pasture and leaped over the rail fence and trotted over to Rosalea and Dawn and pushed his nose between them and nickered softly.

"King!" they both exclaimed, putting their arms around his neck. Pete reached out and patted King's neck.

"Good boy King, you love these girls too, don't you!" Pete said, continuing to pat him.

The cows and calves had been taken care of and the chests of their clothing and things settled in rooms to stay.

The dress donned and the sermon accomplished with the large crew of the riders as witnesses.

King stood near the girls and watched and nickered softly, as though he knew what was happening and putting his approval on it.

The guests, Jonathan and Saraha Brooks and Lilly Obey, would spend the night and would return to Culbert's Crossing the next day.

The 'new life' was beginning for the two young women after the long trip by wagons west to Montana.

Special thanks to

First of all: Thank you Father God, Jesus, my Lord and Savior and the precious Holy Spirit for your help and guidance all of my life and in my writing.

Thank you, my sister Ruby Wallin and my children, my daughters, Della Mae Leftridge and Kandi Kirkland, my sons, Robert (Bob) Renner, John Renner and Arthur (Art) Renner, for encouraging me and pushing me to get the stories published.

God has had a great influence all of my life. In my later years, He has stirred up my desire to write and influenced the writings. So at age 89 my first novel, (A Silver Path) was published. Now at 90 my second novel is being published.

God speaks to me while writing and you will find Him here. God Bless this dear reader with special blessings.